Beck Bear

(Daughters of Beasts, Book 2)

T. S. JOYCE

Novak Grizzly

ISBN-13: 978-1729531952
ISBN-10: 1729531954
Copyright © 2018, T. S. Joyce
First electronic publication: November 2018

T. S. Joyce
www. tsjoyce.com

All Rights Are Reserved. No part of this book may be used or reproduced in any manner whatsoever without written permission, except in the case of brief quotations embodied in critical articles and reviews. The unauthorized reproduction or distribution of this copyrighted work is illegal. No part of this book may be scanned, uploaded or distributed via the Internet or any other means, electronic or print, without the author's permission.

NOTE FROM THE AUTHOR:

This book is a work of fiction. The names, characters, places, and incidents are products of the writer's imagination or have been used fictitiously and are not to be construed as real. Any resemblance to persons, living or dead, actual events, locale or organizations is entirely coincidental. The author does not have any control over and does not assume any responsibility for third-party websites or their content.

Published in the United States of America

First digital publication: November 2018
First print publication: November 2018

Editing: Corinne DeMaagd
Cover Photography: Wander Aguiar
Cover Model: Florian

DEDICATION

For the misfits,
the black sheep,
the ones who don't quite fit in.

You're amazing.

ACKNOWLEDGMENTS

I couldn't write these books without some amazing people behind me. A huge thanks to Corinne DeMaagd, for helping me to polish my books, and for being an amazing and supportive friend. Looking back on our journey here, it makes me smile so big. You are an incredible teammate, C!

Thanks to Travis, the cover model for this book. And thank you to Wander Aguiar and his amazing team for this shot for the cover. You always get the perfect image for what I'm needing.

And last but never least, thank you, awesome reader. You have done more for me and my stories than I can even explain on this teeny page. You found my books, and ran with them, and every share, review, and comment makes release days so incredibly special to me.

1010 is magic and so are you.

ONE

Rhett released the arrow and watched it arching into the woods.

"Did you hear anything I just said?"

Fuck yes, he'd heard every word of Remi's nagging because he listened to everything, but she didn't need to know that. It would only encourage her.

"Do you think I need to manscape more?" he asked, standing up straight and looking down at his bare chest.

"You're as hairless as that damn mole rat you brought home for Raider which, by the way, only has visitation with us every other weekend, so guess who gets to take care of that little bitey monster when he's not around?"

"I'll buy you another one to befriend her, and then you won't have to take care of her. I'll get a boy this time. Oh my god, I just had an epiphany."

Remi's dark eyes went totally dead. "We aren't breeding mole rats."

"Are we not?"

"Stop doing that!"

Rhett loaded another arrow and drew the string back on his compound bow. "Do what?" *Ziiiiiing.* The arrow went sailing into the woods.

"Ask a question every time you don't want to have a serious conversation."

"Why the everlovin' hell would I ever want to have a serious conversation?" He grinned brightly and reached for another arrow off the seat of the green plastic lawn chair Remi had punted into a tree the day she moved here. But he'd fixed it because lawn chairs weren't cheap. They were at least five bucks, and he was poor as shit right now. Plus, he was really good at fixing stuff. *Ziiiiiing.*

Remi was standing there watching him with her lips all pursed, her face all scrunched up and angry, and her black hair whipping around in the wind. She had the coolest hair when it was all wild like this, but again, she didn't need to know that nice stuff. Girls got mushy if you complimented them.

"Did you even brush your hair today?"

Remi shoved him in the shoulder so hard he lost his balance. Stupid grizzlies. So violent. He didn't even try to hide his laughter.

"Rhett Bertrand Finnelfucker, I have a friend coming to visit," she called over her shoulder as she stomped away. "Act right for two days. That's all I'm asking!"

"Polite decline," he called after her as he loaded another arrow. "Also Finnelfucker isn't my last name, but it's kinda cool so I'm gonna change my name. Can you file it with the courts for me?"

"That's not my job!"

"Yes it is! You're supposed to take care of stuff around here."

Remi flipped him off over her shoulder, not bothering to turn around. Four seconds later, the door to her and Kamp's trailer slammed closed.

"Your middle fingers are really skinny!" he called.

"Fuck you, Rhett!" she yelled back.

Hmm. He smiled. He liked the Novak Grizzly.

Feisty, feisty. She was a good fit for this place, and especially for Kamp. That asshole had only gotten into three fights with the Alpha, Grim, this week. Remi was like a little magician.

Damn, he was out of arrows. Now for the challenging part—finding them again. He played this game every week. He shot the arrows randomly into the woods and then went searching for them. Sometimes when it was raining, he dressed like a Viking and set the arrow tips on fire just because it pissed Grim off when he played with fire. Finding the lost arrows settled him. They gave him an excuse to get to know the woods—his territory. Grim and Kamp thought they ran these mountains, but they didn't. The lion inside of Rhett did. He just kept better control of his inner beast. Years of living among the humans had taught him valuable lessons in self-control.

"Why aren't you working?" Grim yelled as he tromped by with his yellow hard hat in one hand and his chainsaw in the other.

"Because I don't want to be?" Rhett offered. Duh, jackass. That answer was pretty obvious. That, and it was his day off. Rhett hadn't had one in two weeks.

Grim snarled and rounded on him. His dark hair was messier than usual and his skin pale as a ghost, his tattoos stark against his pallid flesh. He smelled sick. Not cold or stomach flu sick, but head sick. Or heart sick. The bitter, acrid scent was the same for both. The Alpha looked like he was losing mass in his shoulders, too. Alarm bells, alarm bells. Rhett was the watcher of the Crew. The secret watcher. The jokester everyone ignored, but he paid attention more than anyone realized. Why? Because these mountains and the people here were the only things in the world that belonged to him anymore.

"Are you okay?" he asked, dropping his plastered smile for once.

Grim's bright gold eyes narrowed to slits. "What do you care?"

"Because you're my Alph—"

"No, I'm not. I'm the same as you and Kamp. I wish everyone would fucking stop calling me that."

"Uh, then stop beating us in all the fights," Rhett yelled.

"Then here is my Alpha order." He took a menacing step forward and jammed his finger at the woods. "Get to your machine."

Uh, it really was his day off so Rhett pulled a Remi and flipped him the bird.

Grim launched and snapped his teeth at his finger, damn near bit the thing off. Rhett jerked back just in time. *Thank you lion shifter reflexes.*

"What the hell, man? That's my favorite finger!"

Grim arched his eyebrows unapologetically and walked away, snarling an unsettling sound. He literally might be the worst Alpha in the entire world. Rhett wanted to hate him but, secretly, he admired him instead. Grim was possibly the only one in existence who was more stubborn than Rhett. *I see you, kindred spirit.*

"Have a good day at work!" Rhett called.

"Don't set my woods on fire!"

Rhett chuckled. "Don't give me any ideas."

"I'm serious, Rhett! If I have to come home to another fire, I'm going to kill you and eat you."

Rhett shook his head and made his way for the woods.

Maybe Grim should eat him.

Put him out of his fuckin' misery.

TWO

"Are you good?" Juno Beck's boss asked way too loud into the phone.

Juno hunched her shoulders at the sheer volume of his voice. He knew she was a shifter, so did he have to yell everything? Lord, she could probably hear him from Los Angeles without the phone clutched in her hand.

"Manny, I told you three times already. I'll get to the concert in time. I'm sure the Beefeaters will be super worth our time."

"The Beateaters," he corrected her.

A large man with Funyun breath knocked into her in his rush to grab his suitcase off the airport baggage claim. She pitched forward and had to use the edge of the baggage carousel for balance.

"Sorry," he muttered.

"It's okay," Juno said politely.

"I was talking to her," the man said, pointing to a perfect ten blonde with bright red lips and cat-eye makeup on his other side.

Juno's mouth was definitely hanging open as she watched him tip his baseball cap at the smirking lady and pull his suitcase away.

Rude human.

If he didn't smell like onions, she would've been tempted to eat him.

"Helloooo," Manny said. "Are you listening to anything I say?"

"Yes, yes," she rushed out, lurching forward to grab her own glossy neon-green hard-case luggage. "I'll be at their gig in two days. It's only a four-hour flight from here."

"It's just there are two other record companies circling these guys, and this is the worst time for you to take a couple of days off."

"Well, I haven't taken any days off in four years, Manny, so I think I'm due."

"If we lose these guys, the higher-ups will look at

you."

"Is that a threat? I'm fired if I don't seal the deal? You all use the same threat every time you want some new talent, but guess what, Manny? Most of the people you get desperate for are shit—"

"Excuse me?"

"You heard me. That's why you've sent me out to these dives over the last three months, right? You know I can spot actual talent, but you keep pushing and pushing. You ignore everyone I tell you about and sign these dweebs who sell out in a year, tops. Where is the soul—?"

"In the music industry, blah blah. Spare me your keeping-it-about-the-music bullshit, Juno. Bottom line is money, and talent alone won't get you very far. Look at Linda Lewis. She can't sing a note that isn't autotuned, and her songs are selling by the ton—"

"Because she wears short skirts and no panties on stage—"

"Find me one of those!"

"Manny! No!"

"You were hired to schmooze who we tell you to schmooze. Sign the Beateaters, and we'll talk about giving you a project band."

"A *project* band?" Real talent shouldn't be called a "project band." Juno wanted to reach through the phone and strangle him. She'd worked for years at this soul-sucking job for a chance to sign someone who actually fucking deserved to be signed. She stomped faster past another baggage claim area.

"Juno, you know as well as anyone in the industry, you were hired because of your father. You have to work your way up, just like everyone else."

"Are you serious right now?" she whisper-screamed into the phone as she weaved her way through the busy airport. "You're really throwing who my dad is in my face? I got this job without him even knowing. I've never used his name to build myself up. I hide who I am as much as possible! You degrade the work I've done by saying shit like that to me."

"You have to pay your dues and do the chores that you don't want to before you get your break. Look at what Mark brings us?"

"Mark is a trained monkey!"

"A well-trained monkey who you should take lessons from. He doesn't give me shit every time I send him out on a job. He just gets it done."

"Right, sign Nudist Barbie with three brain cells in her head and be exactly like Mark-the-womanizer-who-sleeps-with-hookers-in-every-town-you-fly-him-to!"

"Juno...sign the Beateaters. I don't care how you do it. They're who the label wants. Do your job and get that band for us."

The phone line went dead, and Juno strangled it while making a screeching sound. A woman looking concerned pulled her toddler closer to her legs, but hang it all, Juno was about thirty seconds away from texting Manny *I QUIT* and calling her career good.

The thing that stopped her? The crinkle of the eviction notice for her condo in her back pocket. She'd read it on the plane after putting it off for the last two weeks. She was upside down on everything. Freaking LA and the ridiculous cost of living.

Her life had turned out so different than she'd planned.

And right now, only one thing in the world could take the sting off her stress level.

And that was one freckle-faced, grinning bestie leaning up against a black F-150 right outside the airport doors. The color of the truck matched

Remington Novak's newly dyed hair.

Juno let off a sigh and blinked back tears as she ran for Remi. It had been way too long since she'd seen her. "Oh my goooosh," she squealed, landing tits-first into her hug.

Juno held her at arms' length just to get a better look at her. Remi's cheeks were rosy, and she hadn't covered her freckles with makeup like she'd done with her ex-boyfriend, Asshole Kagan, as Juno had liked to call him. She'd dyed her hair back to her natural color, and her smile was easy and huge. Her green bear shifter eyes looked even brighter and more animated than she'd seen in years, if she ignored the tears rimming them. "Stop!" she exclaimed. "You know you can't cry alone with me around, and I'm barely holding it together. God, Remi, you look so different. You look...happy."

Remi swallowed hard and cupped Juno's cheeks, studying her face. "You don't."

"Oh, stop," Juno said, angling her face away. "I'm just tired. The flight was long. There was a crying baby."

"You know I can still hear a lie, right?"

"I'm hungry, and I Googled where your new Crew

is. It said something about a cheese factory?"

Remi laughed and threw Juno's suitcase into the back of the truck. She gestured for her to get in. "Let's go, the boys are making you food. We'll have to tackle the cheese factory tomorrow."

"Weeeell, I wanted to talk to you about that," Juno said as she stuffed herself into the passenger's side. "I have to fly out tomorrow afternoon."

"One day?" Remi yelled as she climbed behind the steering wheel. "No, that's not enough. You just got here. Call your boss and tell him to fuck off."

"I tried. The label is going to fire me if I don't sign this band. But bright side, one day together is better than no days, so let's just have as much fun as possible and not talk about work."

"Okay," Remi murmured, pulling out into airport traffic. "No work talk. Only fun." Remi looked over at her with the happiest smile Juno had ever seen on her face. This place had been good for her best friend.

Beaston had told Juno that his daughter could find sanctuary here, and Juno had trusted him. She'd encouraged Remi to come out to these mountains and fulfill some vision Beaston had seen for her. And it had worked.

It was terrifying, because that meant the vision Beaston had had for Juno just might come true, too.

She was going to die soon.

THREE

"Juno," Remi said.

"Mmm?" she answered distractedly as she typed out an email to the administrative assistant of Halfstone Records.

"You're missing it."

"Just a sec..." Juno speed-typed, but made two typos and had to go back and fix them.

"Juno, seriously, you're missing it."

"Missing what?" she asked, looking up at the piney woods blurring by.

"Life," Remi murmured.

Juno sighed. "It's not that simple, Remi. Not for me, not anymore. I have bills to pay."

"It's your day off."

"I don't really get days off. I just have to move those hours somewhere else in my schedule."

The disappointment in Remi's face made Juno's stomach hurt, so she dragged her attention away from her work and stared out the window. "It's really beautiful here. Reminds me of back home in Damon's Mountains."

"How long has it been since you were back?"

"The last time you saw me there. Christmas last year."

"I think you'll like it here," she said softly. "It's really different from city life."

"Do you miss Sacramento?" Juno asked carefully.

"You mean do I miss Kagan, feeling lost, the honking horns and crowded streets, having to worry about where I'll Change, and feeling like a number? No. Not even for a second. I feel at peace here." She cast Juno a quick smile. "I can't wait for you to meet Kamp."

Juno's heart was happy just seeing the joy written into her friend's features. She wouldn't live long enough to find a mate, that much was clear from Beaston's vision. Her end of days was coming up too quickly. But at least she could go knowing Remi had found her place in the world, with the right man who made her glow from the inside out instead of dimming her.

"Why do you look sad?" Remi asked with a little frown furrowing her dark eyebrows.

"I'm not."

"Liar. Since when do you keep secrets?"

Juno shrugged up one shoulder and traded one secret for another to distract Remi. "I totally got another eviction notice on my condo."

"Well, that is the least surprising thing ever. You have to pay like a million dollars for a one bedroom. I don't know how you keep up with the cost of living there."

Juno snorted and checked the email that just came in. "I don't keep up, apparently. My landlord is going to kick me out this time. He ain't bluffin'."

"Maybe that's what's supposed to happen," Remi said so low Juno almost missed it.

"No, that's definitely not what's supposed to happen. I'm not supposed to fail at the one thing I've poured my entire life into."

"Juno, look at your life. You are a puppeteer. An organizer. You got me to these mountains and sent a bunch of strippers to my apartment to get me moving again. You organized for all of my stuff to be brought to Tillamook, Oregon from Sacramento with like...no preparation. And you still kept up with your work. *And* you probably are doing the same stuff for Ashlynn. Am I right?"

Ha, she'd just organized Ashlynn's birthday party in Damon's Mountains from her office hundreds of miles away. "Yep."

"When was the last time you slept for more than four hours at a time?"

"The year was nineteen-ninety-one—"

"I'm serious, Juno!"

"Okay, *Mom*. I don't require a lot of sleep like normies. I'm fine."

"You have bags under your eyes."

"Rude," Juno said, looking up from the email she was writing long enough to give Remi what she hoped was a withering glare. "And besides, eyebags run in my family. It's genetics."

"Brighton Beck doesn't have eyebags, and he's like twice your age. Neither does your mom. Werebears age well."

"I hate when you call us that. We're bear shifters,

not werebears."

"You're the only werebear in existence with eyebags," Remi muttered.

"Oh my Goooood," Juno drawled out, resting her head back and rolling her eyes at the roof of the truck. "What do you want me to say? Huh, Remi? I love my job and I love working and I'm fine. Everything is fine. You said we wouldn't talk about work."

"You don't pick up my calls."

Juno growled. It had been a while since her inner bear cared enough about anything to growl. What did Remi want from her? She was doing the best she could. Lucky Remi, she'd found a good life. A safe life. A good Crew and the perfect mate. It was good for her, but that wasn't Juno's story and never had been. She'd known from age eighteen that her twenty-seventh year on this earth would be her last. And she'd chased a dream with the time she'd had. A mate had never found her, but a passion for music had, probably thanks to her dad, her upbringing, and her hundreds of hours at old bars watching her dad and uncle play to the crowds who would come out to see them. Her fondest memories were of sitting in the studio with the world-famous Beck Brothers, but to her, they were just Dad and Uncle Denny. As an adult? She'd wanted to hold onto that passion and make a career for herself outside of Brighton Beck's shadow. Living in some Crew with the perfect mate wasn't her fate. It was Remi's.

A wave of homesickness took her, but Juno didn't even know for where. Her condo? So she could escape Remi's callouts? The studio she watched all the cookie-cutter bands record the same songs over and over and over? Damon's Mountains?

Had she wasted her life?

Juno, seriously, you're missing it.

Had she wasted her life on this dream?

Juno bit her bottom lip to keep it from trembling and kept her face carefully angled toward the window.

"When are you going to tell me what's really wrong?" Remi asked.

Juno sniffed and forced a smile as she reached for the radio dial. "When I'm dead."

"That's not funny, Juno-Bug."

"Oh my gosh, I haven't heard that nickname in ages."

Remi turned up a gravel mountain road right by a mailbox and pushed the truck higher and higher. "Remember that Halloween your dad actually dressed you like a June bug?"

"I looked like a dung beetle."

"And remember me and Ashlynn begged to match, so our moms had to make the same costumes?"

Juno giggled and set her phone in her lap. "Yeah, and we all looked like a trio of little cockroaches."

Remi was cracking up now. "We thought we were so cute, but our parents took us to that costume contest at Moosey's, and we all tied for Most Disturbing Costume award. We even got those little blue ribbons and everything."

"I still have those somewhere."

"You have mine, too?"

"Yeah, and Ashlynn's. You two always threw everything away so I kept them with my stuff. I had these big plans to make this big scrapbook of our memories."

"Why didn't you ever do that?" Remi asked.

Juno wiped tears of laughter from the corners of her eyes and shrugged. She looked back out the window. At the snow, towering pines, boulders, and uneven terrain. She rolled the window down and inhaled deeply the pine scent, frost, and fresh air. God, it smelled so good here. It really was like Damon's Mountains.

"I don't know," she answered as Remi pulled to a stop in a clearing near an old truck and a navy Bronco. "I guess I just ran out of time."

FOUR

He should rip Grim's roses out of his dumb landscaping just to teach him a lesson. That lesson being "Don't tell me what to fucking do." This happened every time. Rhett had his one day off a week, and every single time, Grim ordered him to work it. He was tired, worn to the bone, grumpy, hadn't been sleeping at nights, and all he wanted to do was go into town and see Sara. It was tradition to see her on his days off, and Grim had been ruining that.

"Rhett, I'm not playing. Get your ass on the processor."

"Fuck. Off. Grim! I'm not taking over Kamp's machine just because he doesn't feel like working today."

Grim's eyes flashed gold in the shadows of his porch. His voice came out a snarl when he said, "It's his day off."

"Welcome to the club. It's my day off, too! Who does the schedule? Because this happens every time."

Grim let off a single, echoing laugh. "Remi makes the schedule. You know, the female *you* brought to our mountains because you thought it would be fun? Maybe you shouldn't have slashed her tires, left mouse traps in their trailer, put chocolate jelly beans in her coffee grinder, *and* bought their kid a motherfucking naked mole rat whose sole purpose in life is to bite everyone. Maybe then she would care about your days off."

"Aaaah!" Rhett yelled. He hated everyone on this mountain. Okay, that wasn't true. He actually secretly really liked them, but they were all getting on his damn nerves today. He needed to Change. And kill something. Or start a bar fight. Or drink all of Kamp's new batch of Pen15 Juice, aka the best beer in Oregon.

His phone vibrated in his pocket, and he snarled at it. All he wanted to do was flip this row of brats and eat a big-ass, greasy lunch, but everyone seemed to need shit from him. He checked the glowing screen.

Fucking Drew with his fucking stalking, perseverance, and can-do-attitude. Rhett had made the biggest mistake in the world the day he'd signed with that money-hungry agent slash manager slash asshole. *This is a new number*, he texted Drew. *Who is this?*

Nice try, Rhett. Where the fuck are you? You were due in the studio three days ago! We have to pay for every day you don't show up. You are in breach of your contract. We are going to sue your ass if you don't deliver. Hear that part clearly! I will ruin you! Cut the shit and call me. Now.

Rhett stared at the fire in the grill and considered throwing his phone in there and cooking it right along with the bratwurst. Thinking of going back to his old life made him want to puke.

Rhett!!!!!

He powered off the phone and shoved it into his back pocket, knowing when he turned it on again, there would be thirty more messages from Drew and the entire staff at the label. And any stalkers who'd discovered his phone number. And possibly members of the Saga Pride. And probably even Benny Ford who he still owed three dollars and seventy five cents to from third grade, because it was his effing luck that everyone in his entire life would need something from him right now.

He just wanted to go see Sara.

Everything would feel manageable if he could just get Grim off his case long enough so he could sneak away. That was one bad thing about being part of a small Crew. When he'd been with the Saga Pride, no one gave a shit if he disappeared for a little while. But here, he always had someone watching him.

He tracked Grim's progress as the Alpha meandered off his front porch, sliding his yellow hard hat over his black mohawk, his gold, suspicious eyes on Rhett. So Rhett graced him with his favorite finger and told him, "Have a good shift!"

When Grim muttered a string of curses and disappeared into the woods, Rhett huffed a little sigh of relief. He burned the tips of his fingers when he pulled the brats off the grill and onto a paper plate. He took a bite of hellfire and did that blow-dragon's-fire out of his mouth while singeing every taste bud, just like all bratwursts should be eaten.

Plate of spicy wieners in hand, he patted his back pocket to make sure he had his truck keys and strode for the trail that led to the parking lot and farther down the mountain. When he spied his rusted-out old Chevy pickup, he grinned because this was it. Escape without the twenty questions from his nosey Crew. Grim was working, Kamp was sleeping in, and Remi, the nosiest Crewmate of all, was in town picking up her friend.

But when he was halfway through the flat field to his truck, he heard it—the soft rumble of Kamp's truck. Mother fucker. Rhett walked faster, but when he tried to open his truck door, it was locked. When his inner lion growled, he didn't even try to swallow it down. Everyone was obnoxious with their breathing and existing and showing up at inopportune moments.

Weiner down! One of the brats had rolled off the plate as he was rushing to dig his keys out of his pocket. "Fuuuuudge pops!" Poor bratwurst. It's only job in life was to be delicious and eaten, and what had happened? It had rolled into the dirt before it had made it to a belly. That was tragedy right there.

And here was Remi, climbing the final ridge in Kamp's big black F150. Stupid jerk had bought a new truck when he started getting paid consistently. And now he was all devoted to making the Crew finish their shifts. Annoying. All Rhett wanted to do was coast by with just enough to take care of his sister. He needed what he needed and nothing more.

"Hi!" Remi called out her open driver's side window.

Crap, now he was going to have to converse with her. "Bye!"

He unlocked the door and set the brats on the seat, but something was behind him. Something big and dangerous. Something that raised the fine hairs on the back of his neck. He turned slowly, and there was a girl. She was tall, only a couple inches shorter than him, and her hair framed her face in perfect golden waves. Her makeup was done up like she was ready for the runway, and she wore a business suit.

She was staring at him with a spark of recognition, a frown drawing down her delicately arched eyebrows. Her eyes were bright silver.

"I found you," she murmured.

Oh, shit. Distract her with insults.

"You found nothing, lady. And why the hell are you dressed for a business meeting? Look around you. You're in the wilderness."

"I know you," she murmured, her frown deepening.

That pissed him off. Pretty girl, but just another nosey person in his life.

He dragged his attention from those striking silver eyes to Remi. "Keep your friend on a leash, Novak. The least you can do is let us keep our privacy here." He tossed her one last dirty look for bringing her fangirl friend out here and hopped up in his truck, slamming the door beside him so hard his rig rocked.

Now he was gonna have a fan all over his life, taking pictures of his trailer and selling information. He bet that in ten minutes she would be all over Twitter, crowing about how she'd found Rhett Copeland. Well, she hadn't found jack-shit. He wasn't Rhett Copeland the country singer anymore. He was just Rhett of Rogue Pride, perpetual fuck-up, and disinterested in anything outside of this little corner of Oregon.

"Rhett!" Remi called as he pulled away.

When he glanced back once in the rearview, Remi looked hurt. Hurt? What had he done? Just asked for privacy. She was ruining everything. How long had it taken him to find sanctuary, and the first thing Remi does is get him busted?

He ripped his gaze off Remi's pout and back to the girl. She was a silver-eyed beauty. With his luck, she probably had a thousand followers on social media. Everything was stupid.

He gunned it and spun the tires on the dirt, zoomed down the mountainside, and didn't look back again.

He was going to have to find a new hidey hole around here. That thought made him feel empty in his middle. As much as he pretended to hate this last-chance Crew, they'd grown on him.

I know you.

Wrong.

Nobody knew him.

FIVE

"What the hell is wrong with him now?" Remi murmured.

Shocked. That's the only word to describe Juno right now. Complete and utter shock. She hadn't in a million years expected to come face-to-face with Rhett Copeland. *The* Rhett Copeland. The young badass of country who wrecking-balled his way through Nashville and hit every award on his debut album. As a shifter! An open-to-the-public shifter. Not only did he have the voice of a motherfreakin' angel, he could rip on guitar and drums, and he'd done more for shifter public relations than just about any other person in existence right now. He'd gotten droves of human women fawning over a lion shifter. A lion shifter! The tide of bitterness toward shifters had turned because he'd blazed a trail, both middle fingers up, no fucks given.

And then he'd disappeared.

Like...people-calling-the-police-filing-a-missing-persons-case disappeared. The world had been playing *Where's Rhett?* for months. Teams of fans were dedicated to searching their towns. His agent was on the news, bullshitting about how he was just in hiding, writing his next album, but any shifter could hear the lie in his answers. He didn't know where Rhett was either.

It had stunned the music industry. First album sold millions, he looked steady on social media, was hilarious, took the sex appeal attention in stride, gave great advice to up-and-coming artists trying to do the same thing he was doing, was the perfect puppet in interviews, well-behaved, and no stories of drinking or drugs ever hit the media. And then he vanished as if he'd never existed at all. And all during a time he was supposed to be recording his second album and releasing some hyped-up single.

The mystery surrounding Rhett Copeland was the biggest gossip and speculation to ever hit the music industry.

And here he was...looking completely different but just the same all at once.

He'd cut off his perfect shoulder-length rock 'n roll hair, and now it was short on the sides and all mussed up on top. He'd given up his clean-shaven look for a short beard that made him look rugged as fuck. Those eyes, though...he couldn't hide those eyes.

Dark blue like storm clouds, but they turned the color of ice when his animal was riled up. Girls would faint at his concerts if his eyes turned colors. There were rumors in the shifter world that he'd trained himself to change the colors on cue instead of only changing when his lion was agitated, just to demolish the ovaries of the swooning girls when he sang.

Every interview that she'd watched, he'd been polite, kind, caring, and as steady as a river.

But he sure wasn't as steady as any river anymore.

"What happened to him?" Juno asked Remi as the taillights of his old pickup disappeared over the ridge.

"Hell if I know. He's always weird, but that was like...angry weird."

"How could you not tell me you are in a crew with

Rhett Copeland?"

"Copeland. I didn't even know his last name …" Remi's eyes went round. "Copeland. That singer dude that went missing?"

"Remington Novak, you didn't know you were in a Crew with motherfucking Rhett Copland?" Juno yelled. "What has happened to your mind, girl?"

"Well, I don't listen to country, and I didn't follow the story. I only heard about it, and my mind has been a little preoccupied with leaving the city and finding a mate and settling here!"

Juno looked around the woods, focusing on one tree and then another and another. Her thoughts were racing a billion miles per hour. Rumor had it his label was about to drop him. Drop. Him! If she could get him to sign with Halfstone Records, she would be on easy street for the rest of her short life. She would make her mark on the industry and maybe, just maybe, not be forgotten in the first year she was cold in her grave. "What do I do?" she yelped.

"Uh, you can unpack your bags and go ATVing with me?"

"No, about Rhett! God, he's really handsome in person. Like…really hot."

Remi scrunched up her face and stared off in the direction his truck had disappeared. "Rhett is?"

"Yeah." Juno's heart was beating too fast. She pressed her fingers against her wrist to check her pulse. Was she going to Change? "That T-shirt clinging to his muscles. He sure didn't let himself go. He's probably put on twenty pounds of mass since he was touring. His eyes are all drop-dead-gorgeous blue, and I could see the line of his pecs right at the top of his loose collar. And that beard. I'm totally into beards. I mean fans. Fans are totally into beards. The world is going to freak out when they figure out he isn't dead in a ditch somewhere! Did you see the way he walks? Like a damn Alpha. Like he could eat anything in his path." Juno let off a little hungry growl. "And did you feel his animal? He's a total Beast."

She ripped her gaze away from the trees to talk about Rhett's sexy fingers, how good they look playing guitar, and how he could probably make a girl come eighty times in a row with those fingers, but Remi was staring back at her like she'd lost her mind, horror written on her face and her skin a little green around the edges. "I'm going to vomit if you don't stop talking about Rhett like that. He is a disaster, Juno. You don't want nothin' to do with that one."

"Not for me! Not for me." She swallowed hard and repeated, "Not for me."

"Who are you trying to convince? Me or yourself?" Remi demanded.

"I meant for the world. For the girls. Fans! He is good for country music."

"Whyyyy?"

"Because he doesn't do that pop stuff. He likes old-school. I mean, yeah, he had to do the sell-out tracks to push his first album, but at the end of each concert, he would sit at the mic and do a cover of one of the greats. Just him out there with a guitar, slaying Hank Williams, Johnny Cash, or Waylon Jennings. And then after each concert, the sales on those songs would skyrocket. He was bringing attention back to good old, down-to-the-roots country." Juno shook her head and sighed. "And then he just…ran."

Remi frowned. "Juno, if he ran, it was for a reason. You can't out him. He's here because he wants to be."

"In a last-chance Crew? That man isn't that damaged. He's fine."

"No, he's really not. He might have appeared

steady on stage, but here?" Remi shook her head. "There are big things wrong with all the males here, my Kamp included. If Rhett doesn't want to be in the limelight, you have to respect that and let him be."

"But—"

"Juno! You aren't here to work. You're here to just...breathe."

Juno huffed a breath of frustration. "You sound like your dad."

"Good," she muttered, yanking Juno's suitcase out of the back of the truck. "My dad knows a thing or two about a thing or two. Maybe for once in your life, listen." She flashed a fiery glance at Juno and brushed past her.

It stung. It hurt, okay? It was hard to watch her best friend since childhood go protective over some guy she'd only known for a few months. He wasn't even her mate either. Rhett was just her Crewmate.

Confused and a little angry, Juno clutched the strap of her purse and followed after Remi. About three yards up the uneven trail, she gave up on her heels and pulled off her shoes. The snow was freezing against the pads of her feet, but not uncomfortable. She'd always loved cold weather, or more specifically, her bear had. Remi didn't wait for her, so Juno crunched her way along the winding trail up the mountain, stepping into the boot prints Remi had left behind. Maybe it was a good thing she had to leave tomorrow. Remi was different and didn't seem to want her around at the moment.

But just as she was making travel plans in her head on how she would get back to the airport, Remi was waiting over the last ridge with a crooked, apologetic smile. "I'm sorry."

Juno came to a stop, her breath freezing in front of her. Shrugging up one shoulder, she asked, "For what?"

"Griping at you. I get all...protective."

"I think that's how it's supposed to be," Juno conceded. "They're your Crew now."

Remi closed the gap between them and hugged her tight, her cheek squished against Juno's. "Yeah, but you'll always be my Crew, too."

Juno huffed at the ache that caused. "I never found my Crew, girl. After I left the Ashe Crew, you and Ashlynn were as close as I could get."

"Why do you keep talking in the past tense? Ashlynn and I are still yours. No matter what life changes we all go through, nothing can touch our history."

"Is this the infamous Juno I've heard so much about?" a tall sandy-haired man with about a billion muscles and the biggest smile Juno had ever seen on a man who had shifter eyes. One gold, one green, and both about as bright as the dang sun.

"All good things I hope," Juno said, laughing as Kamp pulled her in for a hug.

"Oh, hell no, Remi told me all the shit y'all used to get into when you were cubs."

"Oh, God."

"I'm Kamp," he introduced himself, releasing her from his anaconda embrace.

"I figured. I met Rhett already, and Remi told me Grim is a horrible grump."

"Oh, you met the Crew asshole already, huh?"

Juno snorted. "Rhett wasn't so baaaad."

"Liar."

Giggling, Remi pulled Juno toward a trailer park with four singlewide mobile homes. "I have to show you something so cool. I've been keeping secrets, too!"

"What?" Juno croaked, jogging to keep up with

Remi's tugging. "What secrets?"

"Guess who owns these mountains?"

"Uuuuuh, the Alpha? Grim?"

"Nope!! I'll give you a hint," Remi said, jerking to a stop in front of the last trailer on the end. "He's big and breathes fire and his scales are red."

Juno nearly choked on air. "These are part of Vyr's Mountains?"

"Yep! He pays the salaries, posts the numbers to hit, keeps on Grim's ass and everything."

Good God, what was happening? Juno was just staring at Remi with her mouth hanging open, waiting for her to say "just shittin' you." But nope, Remi just grinned back at her.

"But Vyr is a recluse. He said barely two words the whole time we were growing up. He doesn't even like other people. So...why?"

Remi shrugged. "I don't know. He talks to me now on the phone when he needs extra help around here. He seems totally different. Still only talks when he has something to say, doesn't take much shit...and doesn't really joke around very much, but he's different. I think finding his mate and keeping his dragon and stepping out from Damon's shadow have been good for him. And he's with Torren and Nox. I think they've chipped away at him. I think he wanted to help the Crew here. And maybe me, too, I don't know. I think he talks to my dad."

"He talks to Beaston?" Juno whispered. "What does that mean?"

"Can I show her the letter?" Remi asked Kamp, who was standing a few feet behind them.

He gave a soft, crooked smile and pulled a folded piece of paper from his back pocket. "I keep it on me," he said softly.

Frowning, Juno unfolded the piece of spiral notebook paper and read it.

Kamp,

This is hard. You have something of mine, and I don't know you. All I know is what I see. What I dream. I saw you for Remi long ago, right there in those mountains you ruin. Stop ruining. Make a place for her. Take care of her. You've always wanted to make a dad proud. I see it in my dreams. You didn't have that. I will be that. I will be proud, but not now. Not when you fight everything. Stop fighting. Give her Raider. Give her a cub when the time comes but for now, she needs

to breathe. Be. Air.
Beaston

Juno looked up at Kamp, who was scratching his jaw and blinking hard. He handed her another piece of folded paper, and she opened it and read that one, too.

Good Kamp.
Now I am proud.
Beaston

Remi tucked her chin to her chest, and a tear fell to the snow, making a little dark spot right at the toe of her boot.

"Well," Juno murmured thickly, "now I understand."

"Understand what?" Remi asked.

"Why you're so protective of what you've found here."

Remi's smile trembled, and she pointed to the trailer. "I asked Vyr why he put this trailer up here, and he said one word before he hung up the phone."

Juno registered the house number where Remi

was pointing. 1010. Holy shit. It even looked like the old raggedy trailer that had been passed around Damon's Mountains when she'd been growing up. "Let me guess. Beaston?"

"Yep," Remi said. Beaston and Vyr made a sanctuary in these mountains. I don't understand all of what's happening yet. All I know is that things keep falling into place here. I'm putting all my broken pieces back together, and I guess I wanted you to come here and see it for yourself."

"Aww, Remi," Juno whispered, hugging her up tight. "You were never broken. You just needed to find a place that made your heart happy."

"Yeah," she agreed, easing out of the hug to look Juno in the eyes. "And now it's your turn to breathe."

"What do you mean?"

"I got Bash and Ashlynn to hack your airline app. Your flight is cancelled for tomorrow and your account is locked so you can't book any flights for three days."

"What?" Juno barked out, yanking her phone from her back pocket. She opened her app, and sure as shit, it told her the account had been compromised and to call customer service. "Mother fuckers!"

"You can stay in ten-ten this week," Remi said cheerfully, prancing up the stairs with Juno's suitcase. "We'll go start making dinner and give you some time to settle in."

"Remington Novak! What the fuck? I can lose my job!"

"You're welcome!" The door swung closed behind Remi, and Juno had no one left to glare at but Kamp, who stood there smiling with his arms crossed over his chest.

"Don't look at me like that," he said, not even trying to hide his smile. "You know Remi. Once she gets something in her head, she is relentless." He gave her a bro-punch on the shoulder. "Good to finally meet you." And then he walked away whistling. Whistling! They'd just made it even harder for her to get to the dang Beateaters concert and sign those hacks for the label. And he was whistling? Who was going to pay her bills when she lost her job? Huh? Who?

Fuck this. Juno stomped toward the trail that led to Kamp's truck down the mountain. She could hotwire a car, no problem. Another benefit of growing up with the wildling delinquents of the Ashe

Crew. Forget her luggage, she had her purse and her phone, and that was enough. She would go to the airport and fix this herself, get back to life after this emotional roller-coaster of a day.

When her legs locked against the snow, she skidded forward and almost lost her balance. Her purse went flying and hit the ground in front of her. What the hell? She hadn't told her body to stop.

A deep rumbling growl clawed its way up the back of her throat, and when she tried to take a step forward, her body didn't mind her. She took a forced step back instead, and a wave of pain rocketed through her body.

She was definitely, definitely going to Change. Her bear was pissed off, snarling, and she wanted to maul everything. Her skin began tingling with another sign of an imminent Change.

Her stomach hurt, and she doubled over the ache. She couldn't Change. Couldn't! She wasn't prepared and she was somewhere unfamiliar and—

Wait...it was woods. Mountains. Vyr wouldn't have put a bunch of last-chance shifters where they could Change and hurt people easily. Juno gritted her teeth and went to her hands and knees.

A pile of girl-stuff had fallen out of her purse she dropped and lay scattered on the ground. She focused on a half-empty tube of cherry-red lip gloss as the bear ripped her apart.

No, no, no! She was Juno Beck. She'd always had great control over her animal, so why couldn't she stop this now? Fuck!

Pain sizzled through every nerve ending, and a single word blasted through the inside of her throbbing skull. *Want.*

What? "What do you want?" she gritted through clenched teeth to the bear inside of her.

Home.

And then the animal shredded her skin, and all she could see was that tube of lip gloss broken under her six-inch curved claws in the snow. Red lip gloss, white snow, and a bone deep need for...something more.

And then the world went dark.

SIX

"What do you mean she won't see me?" Rhett demanded at the front desk.

"She had a bad night last night, and Dr. Monroe said it's best if she doesn't have any visitors today."

"So it's not her choice but the doctor's? That's my sister. I only get to come here three times a week, if that. Any bad day she has, she can lean on me. Not your entirely human staff who doesn't fuckin' understand what her animal side needs. She needs a Pride. A Crew. And I'm that for her."

Sharon pushed her glasses farther up her nose and shrugged. "I'm really sorry, Rhett. I didn't make the rules."

"Well, you used to be my favorite evening nurse,

Sharon. Now you're second place."

He was pretty sure the lady rolled her eyes, but whatever.

"I want to talk to Dr. Monroe."

"Rhett—"

"Save it," he gritted out. "It took a lot for me to get to come here today, and I got us dinner," he said, lifting the bag of Sara's favorite Barney Burgers in the air. "Plus, she always has a good day after seeing me, and I'm not leaving until you get Dr. Monroe to explain what's actually happening."

Sharon sighed and gestured to the waiting area of the rehab clinic. "I'll page him. I can't promise anything. He's busy tonight, but I'll see what I can do."

"Thank you," he muttered, making his way to the waiting room where he would pace like a caged lion like he did every time they made him wait in here.

"I want to be your favorite again for this," Sharon called.

Rhett snorted and repeated her words, "I'll see what I can do."

One of Sara's favorite nurses waved to him on her way out of the clinic, but he only gave her the head nod as usual. That one tried to flirt from time to time, but he didn't mess around here. This place was for Sara's recovery, and that was it.

Ten minutes of pacing later, Dr. Monroe buzzed himself out of the main doors and gestured for Rhett to have a seat. "Look, I know you're worried, but her bad day had nothing to do with relapse, and she's minding all the rules still."

"Then what happened?" Rhett asked.

"Well, you know how her halfway house closed?"

"Mmm hmm."

"And she did the right thing by her recovery and decided to come back here instead of putting herself on the outside too early?"

"Mmm hmmmmm."

"We gave her limited phone privileges. I didn't see anything wrong with it. She already successfully finished three months here and three months in the house, and she's tough, Rhett. She's doing the work here. It's time for her to start getting little lines to the outside world back so it's not a shock to her when she is released. Or when she checks herself out of here, whatever comes first."

"Okay. So what happened with the phone?"

"The Saga Pride has her number now."

"Whaaaat the fuck?" Rhett whispered, leaning back in his chair. He shook his head, staring at a hairline crack in the wall, wishing he could burn his old Pride to the ground. They were the reason she was in here in the first place. "What are they saying?"

"That they're watching her progress, and your dad wants her to come home and take her place in the ranking."

"That's all well and good except they don't know how to take care of their own."

"*You* feel that way, Rhett. Sara doesn't. She hasn't been in here working on staying clean just for herself. She's been earning her place back in your Pride."

"Not my pride. I left those assholes when they kicked her out. Fuck them."

"Okay." Dr. Monroe ran his hands through his thinning gray hair and sighed. "Let's set up a session for tomorrow, and we can all get to the bottom of this. Because the second she got that message from the Pride, she wanted to check herself out today. I asked her to wait on it, think on it, and she had an unintentional Change in an unsafe situation with other patients here."

"She's in the cage?"

"Just until she Changes back. And it's not like I want her there, Rhett. It's the only form of containment we have so she doesn't hurt or Change the other patients here."

Rhett strangled the bag of burgers and puffed air out of his cheeks, ignoring the growl in his own throat. "Okay. Okay, I understand, and she'll understand too, when she Changes back. She wouldn't ever purposefully hurt anyone, but we understand you have to be safe. And you've taken a risk letting a shifter in your facility. I know you aren't prepared for us. I was just…"

"Just what?"

"I miss my sister, and when I don't get to see her, it's hard on my animal."

"Okay. This is good."

"That this is hard on my animal? Thanks, asshole."

Dr. Monroe snorted a laugh. "No, that you're more open about the process now. Remember the first few weeks she was in here? You were so shut down and fought every step. You were overprotective until you figured out we're here to help. Until you began to trust me and the staff."

"Because I started seeing good changes in her."

"Rhett..." Dr. Monroe opened and closed his mouth like he wanted to say something but couldn't.

"Just lay it on me," Rhett said, relaxing back into the seat.

"I know what you sacrificed to protect her. She told me."

"It's not a big deal."

"No, it really is. I can't name another person in the world who would've done that. And Sharon said you were late on your payment this month."

Rhett ripped the corner of the bag of burgers and rolled it into a ball between his fingers. "My accounts got frozen. I paid the late fees already. I just needed a couple extra days to work so I could cover her stay here."

"What you're doing for your sister..." Dr. Monroe nodded. "Well, I wish more of our patients had support like you. Sara is one of the lucky ones."

"Oh please. She'll always be a dweeb. Tell her I said as much when she Changes back. Can you put these in the fridge and heat them up for her later?" he asked, handing him the burgers.

Dr. Monroe took the bag from his hands and

stood. "Sure. Try back tomorrow. Her Changes don't last more than twelve hours now. She has so much more control over them. Progress."

Rhett huffed a breath and stood to leave. "Yeah, progress. Give her to the Saga Pride, and they'll undo everything she's worked for here."

"You're a good brother, Rhett," Dr. Monroe called after him. "But you can't be her legs forever. At some point she needs to learn to stand on her own."

He understood what Dr. Monroe was saying, really he did. But the doctor was human, and before Sara, he'd only treated a handful of shifters. And none of those were lions. And none of those were the daughters of an Alpha. And none of those had dealt with the pressure Sara had since birth.

It had started snowing again, so Rhett zipped his winter coat up to his neck. He pulled his phone out of his back pocket, and then he called a number he never thought he would've called again. Dad's.

"I figured you'd call," Dad answered. "I know with Sara's return, I'll get you back, too."

"You think so?" he growled.

"Of course. You two are inseparable. Always have been."

"No matter what Sara decides, I'll never be part of a Pride who destroys its own lions."

"If you're talking about Sara, you're wrong. She's stronger than you think she is."

"Oh, I know how strong she is. I'm the one who's here, Dad. I'm the one visiting her, watching her progress, watching her growth. Where were you? Huh? Where the fuck were you when she lost her animal to those fucking drugs you shoved down her throat?"

"I didn't shove any—"

"Bullshit. Seriously, I will call bullshit on every single lie you try to feed me. Give them to your damn Pride. They still have faith in you. I don't."

"I thought I was doing what was best—"

"For you," Rhett snarled. "You wanted a perfect albino lioness princess to sit right beside you and make you look good. And you wanted a perfect albino lion prince to sit at your right hand and wage war on whoever you pointed at. And look at us. I turned singer for the masses, and she got addicted to the shit you gave her. I'm not calling to tell you I'm coming back with Sara. I'm calling to tell you that if she ever gets hurt again, I'll kill you. And you and I both know you can't call bullshit on that. I'm not my father. I don't lie. Guard your neck, *Dad*. Take care of her like you should've always taken care of your daughter, and you'll keep breathing. Screw her up, and I will steal that last breath from you so fucking fast your ghost will stand in your territory for a day, trying to figure out how the fuck he even came to be. Guess how many nights of sleep I'll lose killing you."

He could hear his father swallow audibly over the phone, but he didn't answer.

"Guess the number, and I'll hang up, and you won't have to deal with me until you fuck up again. Guess, *Dad*."

"Zero." His father's voice broke on the word.

Rhett hung up and almost, almost gave into the rage boiling in his veins. He almost, almost chucked his phone against the side of his old Chevy just for the satisfaction of seeing it shatter into a hundred pieces.

He drove the entire way back to the mountains pissed at the world. It wasn't in his nature to stay angry, but as long as he lived, he would never forgive what had been done to his sister. Or to him.

It was dark by the time he turned by the mailbox onto the single lane road leading up to the trailer park. Part of him wanted to go home to his singlewide and drink until he got a song out of him and onto paper, because that's the only way his muse worked nowadays. If he was obliterated, the words came. If he wasn't, he just sat in this life, his feelings building up with no escape until he wanted to drown himself in booze and release all the tension. With a pen. With paper. And with an old guitar his mom had bought him the day he'd told her music sang to his soul. She should've been Alpha, not his dad. She was a queen paired up with a sack of shit who called all the shots in a Pride that would always be stagnant.

He didn't see the bear until it was almost too late. She came right out of the woods and into the road. He locked up the brakes, knowing he would hit her. Knowing it was too late to stop the momentum. The truck skidded sideways, and he saw the fear in her eyes just before he slammed into her. Pretty silver eyes.

He heard the shocked grunt that whooshed out of her, felt her fur through the open window as he lurched to the side on impact.

The truck rocked to a stop, and he winced away from the window, expecting an instantaneous and violent reaction from the she-bear. Grizzlies were terrifying, and even more so when they were hurt.

And from the deep limp she had as she trotted a few steps away from the truck, he'd hurt her.

"Shit," he muttered. "I'm so sorry."

The enormous brown bear had her profile to him, just at the edge of his headlights, staring at him with wide eyes. She looked so scared. Danger. It was dangerous when they were scared.

But he couldn't just leave her out here. The way she glanced around the woods, she looked…lost.

Breath shaking, Rhett shoved open the door beside him and got out slowly, hands up. "Whoa," he murmured when she stood up on her hind legs. She went unsteady on her injured side and fell, barely catching herself on her front paws. She looked from him, to the woods, to him, and back again, as if she wanted to leave but didn't know how.

He didn't understand. She should be charging him right now. Ripping into him for hurting her, but she didn't feel angry to his animal. Just confused.

"It's okay," he murmured, taking another step to her. "It's unfamiliar territory. Juno, right?"

She sat there, tensed like she would run at any

moment.

"You're Remi's friend, yeah? Grew up together or something. I think I heard her say that when I was spying on her and Kamp. I do that a lot. It's boring here, and they talk all the time. Nothing better to do than listen to their blabbering. She said you two grew up in Damon's Mountains together." Truth be told, he was just yammering out loud so it wouldn't be so intimidating to approach an injured grizzly. He cleared his throat and took another step toward her, hands out, head angled, exposing his throat in submission. Did that work for bears? It sure as shit worked for lions. He should've listened better when Remi talked about her people. "You said you know me, right? Rhett Copeland. I used to sing. Now I just fail at lumberjacking and drink a lot of beer. You could say I've found my calling."

The bear snorted and shook her head.

"There we go. You like self-deprecating jokes. Okay. Here's another one. I had everything, and I gave it up on purpose because, believe it or not, living in these mountains with a Crew of fuck-ups is me living my best life."

He was so close to the chuffing bear now. So.

Close. Closer than he'd ever been to Remi's bear without getting claw marks. And Juno's fur was a mouse brown color that waved in the breeze to expose a lighter color underneath. Remi's fur was course and tough, but Juno's looked soft, and he wanted to touch it just to feel the difference. Pretty silver eyes. They looked the same color as the full moon tonight. It was snowing still, so here he stood, his fingers stretching to her neck, snowflakes falling all around them and clinging to the tips of her fur. Heart pounding out of his chest, he touched her fur just light enough to tickle.

She clamped her teeth onto his arm so fast he had no time to react, only freeze and hope she had mercy on him. He could feel her big, sharp teeth putting pressure on his forearm, millimeter by millimeter, and her eyes held him trapped. Or enamored maybe. Did he care if this was his last day on earth? Things had gotten so fucked up. Would it even matter if Juno ended him right now?

Out here in the snow, her powerful mouth on his arm tethering him to her...well, it became a special moment. Her bite was powerful but gentle enough to keep him there. Had he ever been so connected to another living being? For a second, he understood her. Let people close because she wanted comfort, but then punish them when they got too close. How many hundreds of times had he done that in his lifetime?

She clamped down again, just a little more, then released him, and the moment was done.

With a grunt of pain, she hunched into herself and shrank into the form of a naked woman. Juno was all that remained of the beast, her bare shoulders dusted with snowflakes, her hair wild, her knees drawn up to her chest, her thin arms wrapped around them. She was shivering.

"Where am I?" she asked in a hoarse voice.

"Rogue Pride woods," he murmured, yanking off his jacket. He put it around her shoulders, scooped her up, and lifted her from the ground.

"Where are you taking me?"

"Somewhere safe."

"You better not be a serial killer," she said through chattering teeth as he made his way to the truck.

"I'm not a serial killer, but I do like Raisin Bran."

"What?"

"It's a cereal."

There was a split second of silence and then the cutest little laugh he'd ever heard. "That was a really lame joke."

"And yet you laughed. Terrible sense of humor on you."

"You hit me with a pickup truck."

"Yeah, well, that's what you get for recognizing me."

Juno snorted as he settled her into the passenger's seat. "I hope I damaged your truck."

"Oh, you definitely did. We are at war now."

"I let you pet me. We are at peace."

"You tried to bite me. War back on."

She was giggling now, and he froze beside her seat, watching the easy smile on her lips. "Why are you out here without Remi?"

The smile fell, and she cuddled deeper into his jacket. There was that look of confusion again. "I don't...I don't know. I didn't mean to Change."

"You can't control them?"

"If I tell you a secret, will you keep it?"

"If you do me a favor in return."

"I'm not boning you."

"Your loss, but I was thinking you should keep my secret, too."

"Ooooh. A secret for a secret. I tell you something big, and in return for shouldering it, I don't tell a soul you're hiding here."

"Clever bear. Now tell me your secret. I'm pretty good with them. I've learned that Remi is not. She will lay everyone's shit bare."

Juno laughed again. "That she will." She swallowed hard and pursed her lips, searching his face. And then she told him, "I'm supposed to die soon. I think my sickness has begun."

He wished. He wished hard. He wished she would tell him she was just teasing or that he'd heard a lie in her voice, but she was telling the truth. This beautiful stranger believed she would die. "Your secret's safe with me."

"Pinky swear?" she asked, maneuvering her hand out of his jacket to offer one slender pinky.

"Oh, God, I haven't done a pinky swear since fifth grade. I have to remember how to do this." He hooked his pinky onto hers and shook once.

"Rusty, but you'll get the hang of it," she said supportively. "Your secret is safe with me, too.

Whatever reason you have for being here, it's none of my business. Unless you wanted to tell me." She waggled her eyebrows.

"Pass. Now we are at war again." He reached across and buckled her in, then shut the door. The heater worked better when his truck was moving, and he didn't like that she was shivering so much. It dug at an instinct to make her comfortable.

She watched him climb in, shut the door beside him, and throw the truck into gear. She watched him ease his foot onto the gas and straighten out the truck, and she watched him as he guided the rig up the snowy road to the parking field. She definitely watched him as he hummed along to an old Beck Brother's song that floated on the air through the radio.

Her attention never left him, so he stopped humming and asked, "What?"

Juno shook her head and said, "Nothing."

"You're dying. Might as well tell me before you croak."

"Har har." A few seconds of silence went by as he parked his truck by Grim's old navy Bronco. "I look up to you."

"Everyone looks up to me. I'm tall."

"God, you're impossible to compliment."

Rhett sighed and shook his head. "Look, I don't need compliments. I don't even like them. I'm not what everyone thinks. I'm just…me."

"Yeah, the *me* you're talking about? Went against set-list coordinators during an entire sold-out tour and sang acoustic covers of some of my favorite singers at the end of every standing ovation you got. The *me* you talk about didn't ever apologize for being a shifter and didn't hide the animal. The *me* you talk about made me sit up for the first time in years and *feel* country music again. Not just hear it. *Feel* it. That's pretty cool when you can affect people like that."

He sat there dumbfounded as she shoved her door open and got out. His jacket barely covered her butt as she walked barefoot toward the trail that would lead to the trailer park. Long curvy legs that had his dick throbbing, but her words had done something else to his body. His heart was pounding and his muse whispered a lyric for the first time in months without a lick of booze in him.

And then she walked out, the one that got away
I never got a chance to say
after all this time, it's still on my mind...
I wish you stayed...

SEVEN

On the front porch of 1010 sat a chair with a pile of her shredded clothes. Juno's purse was on top of that, all of her stuff tucked neatly back inside. A note had been paperclipped to the edge. The paperclip was supposed to be a dog bone, but looked like a dick when it was attached to something. She laughed. Couldn't help herself. She was still about 35% pissed at Remi for hacking her airline account and messing with her career, but a dick was a dick, and they were hilarious.

She plucked the letter off her purse and read it.

Juno-Bug. You Changed. We saw bear tracks and you totally destroyed your clothes. It's my fault, isn't it? When you get back to the trailer, I swear I will only be a fun friend.

"Yeah? Not the life-ruining kind?" she muttered under her breath before reading on.

I have a surprise. Put some clothes on. You're probably super naked on account of ripping up all yours. That pantsuit was probably expensive, lady. Careful with your duds! Uhhh, don't wear anything expensive tonight, for tonight...we ride! Go change now. I'm watching you. But not in a creepy way. Do you want a hot dog? I made lots. Wait, this isn't a text message. You can't respond. I'll just bring hot dogs. Okay, go put underoos on. See you soon, bye.
-Remi, Your Awesome Amazing Not Annoying Heart In The Right Place Good Intentioned Friend

Juno growled, but it came out human. Oh, now her bear wanted to hide?

Juno sighed and wondered how the hell she was going to tell Remi what Beaston had predicted. She was scared. Okay? She was terrified by what had happened tonight. Juno folded the letter and pulled her purse off the chair, made her way to the door. She was scared of dying. Scared of these first signs of sickness, scared of losing control and being remembered for her death, not her life.

At the door, she turned just in time to see Rhett come out of the tree line and make his way to the trailer next door. He had on a white thermal sweater that had a V at the neck and showed off those pecs of his. The man had probably boned more girls than he could count.

"Stop looking at me like I'm a hamburger, Juno. If you wanted to eat me, you missed your chance."

"I tasted you," she teased. "You taste like beer and bad decisions. I spat you back out."

His chuckle was deep and gravelly and, yeah, it was sexy, too. Annoying. "Bad decisions, yes. I've actually patented a cologne with that scent. But beer? Nah. I haven't had one yet today."

"Yet."

"About to change that right now. Night Juno." His frosty blue eyes stayed on her until he disappeared onto the porch of his trailer.

A few seconds later, she heard the plucking of guitar strings. God, he was so good. So natural. So enthralling. She could've stood out there listening all night if it weren't for the freezing weather and her lack of "underoos," as Remi had put it. Why was she so dang cold tonight? Oh yeah...because she was getting sick. Which wasn't fair because shifters rarely even got sick. Normal shifters were born healthy and died of old age. And here she was, twenty-seven years young, and her days were numbered? She kind of wished Beaston had never told her this stupid destiny. She got it; he didn't want her to waste her life. Because of his prediction, she'd worked harder, had slept less, got more done but, good God, what did a real day off even feel like? Like this? Like an emotional roller coaster that revolved around work, guilt over not working, or thinking about work?

For the first time in her career, she wished she could just forget everything for a little while.

Dress warm. And cheap. That was what Remi had basically told her in the letter, so she pulled on some skinny jeans, her pristine Ugg snow boots with pretty lace ribbons in the back, a tank top, and a white sweater. She turned this way and that in the mirror. Huh. She looked pretty good if she ignored the skinny jeans being a size too small and squeezing her butt fat upward into a muffin top. Which she actually didn't ignore, because the tops of muffins were the yummiest part.

An engine revved outside, and Juno grinned at herself in the mirror. Yep, tonight she was going to play and ignore all her worries. She grabbed her jacket and jogged out of 1010 to the edge of the porch.

Remi and Kamp were each on mud-splattered four-wheelers.

Remi held two hotdogs in the air. "Get on the back, bitch. Tonight, we ride."

"Doooo we call each other bitch now?" Juno asked in a high octave.

"All the kids are doing it. Rheeeeett. Rhett," Remi called with her tongue sticking out. Dear goodness, was she drunk? "Rhett, Rhett, Rhett, Rhett, Rhe—"

"What?" Rhett yelled, throwing open the door to his trailer. "What, what, what, WHAT?"

"Whoo, your eyes are really blue," Remi said through an unapologetic grin. "Come play with us. We tried to get Grim, too, but the Reaper is in the woods again. You're our second choice. Come on."

"No spanks, Novak." He disappeared back inside his trailer.

"There is beer involved, and Juno's tits will be smashed against your back," Remi said at normal volume.

And like magic, Rhett reappeared and jogged down the stairs. "Like I was saying, I'd love to come play."

"Wait, what is happening with my tits?" Juno asked as she watched Remi dismount and let Rhett have her spot.

"Your tits, my back," Rhett said, revving the four-wheeler and waggling his eyebrows. "Smash 'em."

While Remi was crawling onto the back of Kamp's four-wheeler, he was cracking up, discouraging her to, "Stop eating Juno's hot dogs." And, indeed, her best friend in the whole wide world was inhaling Juno's dinner. Rude.

Juno stomped over to her, yanked the one remaining un-maimed hotdog out of Remi's hand, and angrily took a bite before she hoisted her leg over the back of Rhett's four-wheeler.

Rhett yanked the jacket out of her hands and tossed it up on the front porch.

"Hey!" she exclaimed. "I'm cold."

"You're a werebear," Rhett muttered. "You'll

survive."

Seriously, he called them werebears, too? Ugh! "Dying, remember?" she growled against his ear.

"Holy fuck, keep doing that, but whisper something sexier than 'dying.' That word is a boner-killer."

She leaned forward and purred, "Venereal disease."

"I don't like this game, zero stars, do not recommend," Rhett muttered.

Remi leaned over and almost fell off Kamp's ATV to hand Juno a flask. "This'll warm you up!"

Juno shook it gently. "It's almost empty."

"Whoopsie." Remi giggled and then cleared her throat primly. "Rules of the game—there are pink markers on the trees. Follow the markers to each checkpoint where there will be a puzzle. Before completing each puzzle and moving on to the next check point, we each must shotgun a beer."

"Fuck, yes," Rhett said. "This is literally the only cool thing you two have ever done."

"Not polite," Remi said, pointing to him. And then Kamp hit the throttle and spun out, spraying snow all over Rhett and Juno. Her cackling laughter echoed through the clearing as Rhett hit the gas. Juno yelped and barely got her arms around his waist before she fell off the back.

"Hold on tight, but also drink that flask."

Her voice shook from all the bumps as she said, "Uh, pass. I'll spill it on my sweater."

"So?"

"It's white."

"Make a stain, Juno! Make a memory!"

And she got it. Smudge that perfect sweater and remember this night when she went to wash it. Or if the stain stayed, always remember it. Chest heaving with excitement, she said, "Okay! But keep it steady so I don't choke!"

"That's what she said," he called over his shoulder.

Juno laughed into the flask and choked anyway. Dirty boy. When she recovered from coughing, she downed the rest, only spilling a few drops down her chin and onto her sweater, and then she tossed the flask on the ground just at the edge of the clearing before they hit the tree line. Rhett's waist was taut like a Grecian statue. Boy had been doing his core workouts, yummy. And he smelled good. *Sniff, sniff.*

Cologne. Maybe he really had made a cologne called Bad Decisions. His triceps were all flexed against his tight white thermal sweater. They both matched. White sweaters. So cute. Up ahead, she could see Kamp and Remi's taillights. Rhett was good at driving and catching up fast. Juno gave a belly laugh when the wind whipped against her face.

"God, you have a great laugh," Rhett called out.

"Aw, what a sweet complime—"

"And great tits."

Juno rolled her eyes heavenward, but really, she was flattered. It had been a while since anyone had paid attention to those.

"There's a marker!" she yelled, pointing to the pink plastic ribbon tied around a tree. "And another way up there! See it?"

"Yep, I see it. Good eye." The little engine roared as he hit the throttle and took them into the woods.

Juno squeaked and held on tighter as he wove in and out of trees, ten yards off the trail. They were neck and neck with Kamp and Remi now. Remi was still laughing like a psychopath and waving a half-eaten hotdog in one hand while holding on to her mate with the other.

Juno was cracking up now, because how long had it been since she'd seen her friend like this? Since she'd seen Remi full of pure, undiluted joy? It was infectious.

"Here we go," Rhett murmured, kicking it into the next gear. He cut in and slid back onto the trail right in front of Kamp.

Juno squeaked and expected to crash at any second, but when she eased her eyes open, they were passing a second pink marker, and up ahead was a lantern and a hand-painted sign that said *Stop Here Asswipes*. Lovely.

Rhett hit the brakes hard, and they skidded to a stop. He jumped off just as Remi and Kamp slid to a halt beside them. Rhett held out his hand and helped Juno off, then they ran for the puzzle. He didn't let go of her hand. He didn't let go. She stared at their intertwined fingers as they ran, boots crunching in the snow, his big strong hand pressed against hers. So warm. So safe.

There were beers sticking out of the snow. It was a redneck cooler, ha. When Rhett let her hand go to pick up two of them, there was a little moment of disappointment. She'd liked that connection.

Rhett pulled a knife from his back pocket and flicked it open smoothly, as though he'd done it a hundred times before. And maybe he had. He tipped the first blue can on its side, cut a slice near the bottom, widened the hole with his thumb, and handed it to Juno. "Okay, you need to pull the tab at the same time you—"

Juno popped the tab as she put her mouth on the hole and threw it back. She gulped until it was done, spilling some down her face, and for a second, Rhett stood there with his eyes wide, looking amazed. He brushed a thumb across her chin, tracking the movement with his eyes as he murmured, "You are the perfect woman." And then he did something that shocked her into complete stillness.

He kissed her.

Just...leaned in and pressed his lips against hers, held for a three count before he brushed his tongue against her bottom lip and sucked gently. And for those few seconds, Juno just was. She just existed. No problems, no cares, no worries over her future, just lost in a kiss with a sexy man.

He ended it all too soon. His hands gripped her waist and he eased back, looking as confused as a man could possibly look, eyebrows lowered over fiery blue eyes as he searched her face. "Temptress," he murmured.

Breath shaking, she wanted to whisper something profound that would bind his heart to hers, but all that came out was, "I shotgunned a beer."

Well, that broke the spell. Rhett laughed and released her waist. "Yeah, if you ever want this dick, just pull out the Bud Lights. Apparently, I'm that easy. Now stop distracting me. We need to win, and I can't focus with your lips all pouty and cute and delicious looking."

"Ha! Your turn, hurry! Pop that top." She glanced at Remi and Kamp, but if they'd witnessed their little smooch-fest, she couldn't tell. They were already doing their puzzle, twin frowns on their faces as they stared at a pile of wooden shingles with numbers painted on them.

Rhett shook his head hard as though trying to clear it, cut his can, and tipped it up, popping the top as he did. Beer spilled down his face like it had hers. She was grinning like a crazy person by the time he took his sleeve and wiped it across his chin, then tossed his empty can in the snow next to hers and tugged her toward the puzzle. It was a brain teaser with a pile of different numbers scattered in the snow and a sheet of directions. There was a wooden board with five empty rows, and they had to put five of the numbered pieces on each row that would add up to sixty-nine.

"I'm really shitty at math," Rhett muttered when they were finishing the second row.

"I'm not!" The numbers clicked in her mind, and Juno pulled the remaining pieces from the pile and arranged them on the last three rows. "The fifteen goes on the end of that one!" she exclaimed, directing him. Remi and Kamp were at the same pace as them.

"Wait, this isn't really that fair," Juno shouted as she and Rhett raced for the ATV. "Remi and Kamp arranged the puzzles!"

"Nope! Grim did!" Remi called as she stumbled in the snow. She barely caught herself and then jogged toward her ATV.

"Grim put this together?" Rhett asked, but his voice was so soft Juno thought he wasn't really asking anyone in general. Just himself.

"Is that weird?"

"Grim doesn't play games. Or socialize with us in

general. Or do anything nice."

"Oh. Well, what does he do?"

"Yell and kill things."

"Oooooh," Juno said, disturbed at the description of this Crew's Alpha. "Y'all are super fucked-up."

"Amen!" He hit the throttle and swerved in front of Kamp, hitting his bumper with the back end of their ATV. When he glanced back over his shoulder, he was grinning from ear to ear. And his smile was stunning. Perfect, straight, white teeth and those glowing blue eyes. The scruff on his chiseled jaw, muscular neck, hair all windblown...the stage lights and cameras hadn't done this man justice. In real life, he was even better.

By the third checkpoint, Juno was feeling the buzz from the drinks. She was giggling more and stumbling over the puzzles. Were they getting harder? Rhett was encouraging and supportive, telling her "Atta girl!" any time she helped their little team. On this one, it was cornhole, but they had to each throw in three beanbags in a row into the tiny holes on the boards before they could move on. She thought they would never get it because she kept throwing two in a row and missing the third. But they did and were somehow still neck-and-neck with Kamp and Remi. This was the last of the race, the final leg, so when Rhett hit the brakes and let Kamp pass them, she was confused.

"What's wrong?" she asked as he stopped on the trail.

He pointed to a set of lion tracks in the snow. "We're being hunted. Grim didn't set this game up. The Reaper in him did."

Up ahead, Kamp had slowed to a stop and looked back at Rhett, a warning flashing in his gold and green eyes. Whatever they said with that look, Juno didn't know, but Kamp turned his ATV around and murmured something low to Remi. Rhett pulled Juno's hands tighter around his waist. "We're gonna finish the race up to the trailer park, sound good?"

"Wait, we aren't finishing the game?"

Rhett didn't answer, and as he turned the ATV, the headlights caught a reflection of animal eyes off in the trees. "Shit," he murmured, gunning the four-wheeler so fast she left her stomach back on the trail. "Hey Juno? If I stop this ATV, you and Remi finish the race."

"What do you mean?"

"I mean, if me and Kamp get off the ATVs, you stay on and don't look back. You just get to the trailer park." He cast a tight smile over his shoulder. "You win for us, okay? Win or we're at war again." He was teasing, but his voice sounded so serious, and whatever he saw when he looked behind them furrowed his brow with a frown.

And then she felt it. A wave of dominance, something big coming for them. She almost didn't want to look back, almost didn't want to know, but she thought to herself that imagining what was behind them would be way worse than actually seeing what was behind them.

She was wrong.

A massive, black-maned, scarred-up lion was charging them full speed and gaining on them. His face was snarled up with hatred, and his eyes glowed as yellow as the sun. His enormous paws and powerful, relentless stride catapulted him closer and closer to them.

"Oh my gosh," she whispered. "Is that Grim?"

"No," Rhett answered. "That's the Reaper. Grim isn't home tonight."

Rhett never let up on the throttle through the

turns, he never slowed, and he stayed right on the tail of Kamp's quad. It was like a dance. A terrifying dance where both ATVs skidded to the side on turns together, spraying snow, and straightened out in unison. The boys could ride. But Juno was on the back of the second one, which meant the Reaper was going to eat her first. She could hear him now, his paws hitting the snow, his breath, his snarl. So close, she didn't want to turn around and see her death coming. Something was wrong with him. So very wrong. He felt off. Dominant and sick, but not physically ailing...more like head sick.

"I need to Change," she cried as she felt the first wisp of his breath on her back.

Rhett tensed under her embrace and said, "Go home!"

And then time slowed. Rhett leapt up in the air, arching his back, Changing mid-air above her, his glowing blue eyes locked on whatever horror was coming for them. She ducked as an enormous, snow-white lion exploded from him right in the middle of his graceful arch over her and screamed when he landed on the Reaper behind her with such force it blasted through her. Without Rhett at the handlebars, the quad slowed. She should Change and help him. Another lion with a tawny coat and sand-colored mane bolted past her stalling four-wheeler. Kamp.

Juno lurched forward and grabbed the handlebars to keep it steady, and behind her, the sounds of a snarling, roaring lion war was deafening. They slapped and dragged their claws down each other's bodies and sank their long teeth into their hides like they wanted to kill each other.

"Juno!" Remi screamed. "Let's go!"

"But—"

"No buts, the boys told us to go home. This is between them." The sound of her engine ripped through the roaring of the lions.

Juno hesitated a moment later, allowing the ATV to coast to a stop. She sat there stunned at the sheer aggression the fun-loving Rhett was capable of when the white lion took his body. He was every bit the size of Grim and layered with muscle, the striations showing with every powerful slap of his paw. His lips were pulled back over his impossibly long teeth. If ever violence had been poetic or graceful, it was here in the Rogue Pride Woods.

The Reaper broke free of the battle, and his eyes

locked on Juno. He was coming for her. With a yelp, she hit the throttle and fled behind Remi. Maybe she would have ignored the boys and Remi's instruction and fight alongside them if she trusted her bear. But right now, she was sick, and when she'd Changed earlier, she'd only been confused and lost and didn't remember most of her time in the woods. She couldn't trust her animal to be of any help right now. All she could do was what Rhett and Remi told her to—run.

The ride back to the trailer park was terrifying. Not for her own safety, but she kept remembering Rhett as he'd been the last seconds she'd seen him, clipping the Reaper's legs out from under him and biting down on the monster's back leg. He was trying to buy her time, but what would be the repercussions for him? Hurting his Alpha like that. He was fearless, but at what cost?

By the time she pulled the ATV to a stop beside Remi in front of 1010, her heart felt like it would jump right out of her chest.

"Why did he do that?" she punched out through ragged breath. "Why did Grim attack us?"

"I told you," Remi said in a sad voice. "The males

here are all damaged. Grim is the most damaged of all. He has two lions. Grim and the Reaper. The Reaper is stronger, but he's also a killer. They call this a last-chance Crew for a reason Juno. The Reaper is the main reason. Kamp and Rhett have to fight him, and someday soon, they'll put him down. That's the cost of settling in this Crew. We have a shot at happiness during the day, but we pay in blood at night." Remi dismounted and shook her head, her eyes on the woods. "Welcome to my world."

Rhett had told her not to look back, but that was impossible to do. Inside, her bear was awake, eyes on the woods, worried.

Remi sat on the porch of 1010. Juno wiped new snow off the bottom stair, sat on it, and leaned back against her friend's knees.

And together they waited for the lions to come home. *Home.* Juno huffed a soft breath. She hadn't called a place home in years. She travelled too much. But she was probably just thinking that way because Rhett had said, "Go home."

1010, Crew battles, fun drinking games, and everything did feel familiar—like back when she was growing up in the Ashe Crew. She'd had more fun tonight than she could remember having. Her sweater was probably ruined into a memory, like Rhett had said, and the toes of her gray fashion Uggs were splattered and stained darker from the melted snow on the tips.

But, tonight, she'd felt alive.

And for a split second, sitting here waiting on a man to come home, she imagined her life like this, if only she were able to continue living. To continue breathing. Beaston had told Kamp in that letter to be air for Remi. Be. Air.

And deep inside of Juno, she wished for that, too.

It was silly, she knew, but as she rested her fingertips on her lips where he'd kissed her, she wished for Rhett to be her air.

EIGHT

Fuckin' Grim. Couldn't help himself, could he? Couldn't let them have one fun night without fuckin' it up and bleeding everyone. And if he'd caught up to Juno? Rhett spat in the snow and wiped the seeping blood off his ribcage for the tenth time since he'd started his trek home. He had almost killed Grim tonight. Maybe that's what that psychopath had wanted. To be put down. If he'd gotten a single claw in Juno…

"Hey, wait up," Kamp called, his voice echoing through the woods. His bootsteps were crunching in the snow behind him faster. There was the one benefit to being a lion shifter—they shredded all their clothes during a Change, but their paws slipped right out of their boots. "About the only thing I can keep," Rhett grumbled.

Rhett stomped his naked ass faster because Kamp was catching up and he didn't want to talk to anyone right now. He just wanted to hike up to the trailer park and see if Juno was okay.

"I saw you kiss her," Kamp said, drawing up beside him.

Look at the pair of them. Butt naked except for work boots, having a nice winter's walk through the forest, both dripping blood. Juno was right. This Crew really was fucked up.

"My life used to be so simple," Rhett gritted out, shoving Kamp away. "And stop walking so close to me! I swear to God if your dick touches me, I'm burning down your damn trailer and setting Waffles with Peanut Butter free."

"Okay, first off, I'm not trying to touch you with my dick! It's just big."

Rhett snorted. Cocky asshole.

"And second, I'm still about forty percent pissed that you bought Raider that rabid fucking naked mole rat, and third! Rhett, I know you heard me. I saw you kiss Juno."

They stumbled over the last ridge before the trailer park. "So what, man?" Rhett said, breath freezing in front of him as he rounded on Kamp. "I can't kiss a girl? It didn't mean anything."

"Lie," Kamp said softly, resting his hands on his hips.

Rhett growled and shook his head in a warning. "Kamp, if you don't cover up your stupid dick right now—"

Kamp cupped himself and arched his eyebrows like *better?*

No. No. No, no, no, nothing was better! Now his head was all messed up on a girl he barely knew. He couldn't stop thinking about that damn kiss, the sound of her laugh, her silver eyes, how startled her bear had looked when he hit her with his truck, or the way she stared at him in the passenger's seat while he hummed a song. Like he fuckin' mattered. Like he *mattered*. Or the way she'd said she looked up to him. Or the way her smile was higher on one side or the way her eyes crinkled at the corners as though she'd spent her whole life laughing. Or how much fun it was to have her holding onto him while he drove that ATV like a madman through the woods, just to test her, just to see if she would tell him to slow down.

"My life is complicated," Rhett said. "Juno will leave soon, and we'll all go back to normal."

"None of this is normal," Grim said.

Rhett and Kamp both jumped and took a few steps back from the Alpha, all bloodied up and leaning against a tree as if he'd been there the whole time. Birthday suit and boots. Nothing like Rogue Pride bonding time. Rhett hated everything. Except Sara. And Juno. They were cool.

"I saw you kiss her, too," Grim said, his eyes blazing yellow still as if his lion was still in control. Problem was, they could never tell which of the two lions was in charge at any given time. Grim? Or the Reaper.

He looked completely at-ease except his black mohawk was messed up. He was scary quiet when he wanted to be.

"Good for both of you. You have eyes in your head." Rhett turned and walked away, flipping them the bird over his shoulder.

"She's Remi's friend," Kamp called.

"So?"

Kamp sighed. "So don't ruin her."

Rhett rolled his eyes to the clouds above and shook his head. Assholes. Like Rhett intended to ruin her. Sure, he was always trying to get out of work and laid out boobytraps in Kamp's trailer when he got bored. And sure he'd put Pen15 Juice labels on all of Kamp's beer and sold it without his permission. And sure he hid the mail from the Crew, slashed Remi's tires, and bought Raider a naked mole rat mostly to piss Kamp off, but he was *mostly* a good person.

His beer buzz had worn off and his ribs hurt like a motherfucker. He was cold down to his soul and had work early in the morning. Which he needed to figure out how to ditch so he could have visitation with Sara and Dr. Monroe.

But all that fell away as he looked up and saw her—Juno.

She was sitting on the bottom stair of 1010, huddled in her jacket that she must've picked up from the porch where he'd thrown it, shivering, elbows resting on bent knees, cheek resting on her hand, windblown golden hair lifting in the cold breeze, silver eyes steady on him.

The first time I saw you I knew,

You would be the end of me
And I didn't want to lose,
Everything I thought my life would be
I fought you from the second I knew you...
From the second I knew you...

He could hear the guitar chords as the lyrics came to him.

Hello again, muse.

Remi jogged past him to get to Kamp, but he barely registered her. He couldn't take his eyes off the worry that pooled in Juno's eyes. How long had it been since anyone had worried over him?

Felt nice. Better than nice... For some strange reason, it was a relief to have one person care about his well-being for once. Not because he was a singer. Not because he had a big following. Not because of *what* he was, but because of *who* he was. He didn't care what Kamp and Grim said. She was here for a day, or two days, or a week. She was temporary, but he wanted to keep this feeling of connection. Like the moment she'd clamped her teeth on his arm and held there—just existing, two bodies turned to one. That hadn't gone away. In fact, it had gotten stronger with their kiss. He couldn't take his eyes off her, even when she wasn't around, if that made any sense. She felt different than other people, and he'd met thousands. He'd become desensitized to people, and here she was, pulling feelings from him he'd thought he was incapable of.

He didn't know why she was so interesting to him, or why he was so attracted to her. All he knew was that he didn't want to get rid of this feeling and cut her off just because the others thought he ruined everything he touched.

She was waking up his muse, so maybe he would ruin her just a little.

He was okay being a stain if he could make a good memory for her.

NINE

The relief that flooded her veins had Juno sighing the breath she hadn't even realized she was holding. The second Rhett came out of those woods, his gate steady and strong, she felt dizzy with how glad she was that he was all right.

He'd protected her. Her. A big old bear shifter. Yeah, she was submissive, and fighting was hard on her animal, but he hadn't known that. All he'd known was that he was going to take care of the threat, and she needed to get somewhere safe.

Good man.

She frowned. Injured man. He was coming straight for her, and as soon as he stepped into the halo of porch light, she winced. The left side of his torso was all clawed to hell. But if he felt the pain, his cocky, crooked smile hid it. His shoulders were wide and cut and his abs on full display, flexing with every step in the snow. He wore tan work boots that were still unlaced and nothing else. Dayum. There should be, in existence, a twelve-month calendar of just men in boots and nothing else. She was trying not to stare at where his big hand cupped his nethers but, good lord, it had been a while since she'd seen a man like this. No, strike that. She'd never seen a man like this. She wanted to say something smart, but once again she fucked up the moment. *Say I like your shoes. No, say I like your nipples. No, don't do that. Be cool. Say—* "I like your shipples." *No!*

She squeezed her eyes closed and hung her head as his deep laugh echoed through the clearing.

"Thanks? I think?"

"Yeah, well, if you ever need a moment turned awkward or a weird compliment, I'm your girl."

"Mmm, you're my girl, huh?" he asked so softly she nearly missed it over her own embarrassed giggling.

"What?" she asked, hope blooming in her chest.

"I want to show you something."

"If it's your dick, I can actually see it right now, peeking through your fingers," she said, pointing.

"Ha!" he said, looking down and adjusting his hand to cover more. "I mean something not perverted, but thanks for keeping us in the awkward stage."

"I've had a lot of practice," she said, bowing her head once.

"I would guess a lifetime of practice."

"You would be correct. Okay, show me your non-penis. I'm super prepared."

Rhett twitched his head toward 1009. "It's in there."

"Are you about to get creepy?"

"I'm not luring you into my den, Juno. You know who I am, or I guess...what I was. It's one of the only things I brought from my old life."

Intrigued, she stood and called out, "Night, Remi, I'm going to a slumber party at Rhett's tonight."

"Cool, don't get an STD," Remi called.

"What the hell, Remi?" Rhett drawled out. "Shifters don't even get those and thanks for the cock-block."

"I'll kill you if you touch her," Remi sang out as

she and Kamp headed back toward their trailer, arms around each other's waists.

"Hate," he muttered low to himself as he lead Juno toward his trailer.

Juno was really trying to hide a smile, but it wasn't working.

"Glad you're amused," he muttered.

"I owe you an apology," Grim said from Rhett's front porch right as they moved to climb the stairs.

"Aaah!" she and Rhett both yelped in unison, jumping back like a pair of synchronized swimmers who had practiced the move a hundred times.

Grim was sitting on the plastic chair, staring at them like they were steaks and he'd skipped dinner.

"How the fuck did you get up here?" Rhett asked.

Grim ignored his question and said, "I'm sorry I almost killed you tonight."

Rhett looked down at her, but hell if she knew who Grim was apologizing to. She was pretty sure his lion tried to kill everyone here tonight.

"Uh, there's always tomorrow," Rhett muttered as he grabbed her hand and led her to the front door.

The snarl that emanated from Grim's throat lifted the hairs on the back of her neck. But he shook his head hard, said something to himself she didn't understand, and stood to leave. Rhett pulled her into the house and locked the door behind them.

"He means well," Rhett said.

"Really?"

"No."

She snorted a laugh. Okay, most of today shouldn't be funny, but he had a way of lightening any situation. He was funny. "Just so you know, a sense of humor ups a boy's hot-points by at least a dozen."

"Only a dozen? That's my only positive attribute."

"Exactly, so your hot-points are at twelve."

He snickered and led her through the small kitchen to a back bedroom. She was about to pop off again about how she really wouldn't be licking his pickle tonight, but she swallowed her words down when she saw why he'd brought her in here. In the back corner of the room, hidden from easy view by a bed, there was a single guitar on a stand. Oh, she recognized it. Any girl who claimed to be a fan of his would. It was an old beat-up Martin acoustic guitar with a soft leather strap where he'd hand painted the words *Country will never die.*

The frets were all worn, and the fretboard scuffed from pressing strings on it for so many years. The thing was scratched and had a strip of camouflage duct tape along one curve. The pickguard was black and had been scuffed all to hell.

This instrument had seen music.

Real music.

"Someone special gave me that when I was sixteen," he murmured, pulling on a pair of sweats. He disappeared in the bathroom for a few seconds and returned with a dark gray towel, pressing it against the worst of his claw marks on his ribs. He tossed the bloody towel into the hamper in the corner and picked up the old guitar by the neck. He sat on his unmade bed, his leg dangling off the side, the other folded under him. He plucked it distractedly.

"Perfectly in tune," she murmured, closing her eyes at the notes. God, she'd missed the simplicity of plucking strings. When she opened her eyes, he was looking at her so strangely.

"What?" she asked.

Without a word, he shifted positions and put the guitar in her lap. She took it from him on instinct, her fingers finding her favorite chord, her right hand stroking the strings. Her heart heaved a sigh with happiness.

"Play," he demanded.

She strummed a few more chords and plucked out a melody to one of her dad's old songs he wrote for her mom. She messed up twice and replayed it until she had it committed to memory again. "It's been years."

"Don't matter. Ain't nobody here but us, and you've already impressed the shit out of me."

So...she played, but she didn't sing because she would cry. Happiness did that to her sometimes, made her eyes leak all the emotions she failed at keeping inside.

And holding this old soul—this old guitar—this possession that had known more love than most people, that had known more devotion just from a set of fingertips...well, it broke something inside of her. But the breaking didn't hurt. Sometimes when a dam flooded during a rainy season and the water pushed and pushed, rose higher and higher, the dam might feel the break but, oh, the water—the water was free.

Juno hadn't realized it, but she'd been in a rainy

season for way too long.

And Rhett had just placed a crumbling dam in her hands.

Instead of singing, she would reward him for sharing this with her. She would share, too. So as she played, she told him a story.

"When I was a girl, I spent so much time in bars. I remember watching my dad play at this local place with my uncle. I would be doing my homework up at the bar with this nice bartender there named Layla, my mom helping me. And always, *always*, there was music in the background of my life. I can't count the times I fell asleep in my mom's lap at the late shows. And she would ask me, 'Juno, why don't we stay home tonight so you can sleep in your bed?' And I would always say the same answer. 'Because I never want to miss a show.' When we were home, my dad was on his guitar, and he never told me to go away so he could write his songs. I was always just…there. That was my life. I had the best childhood. He can't talk well, only whisper, but he would say that music was in his blood, and he'd given that to me. One day I came home from school, I was maybe seven, and he had an old secondhand guitar he'd bought at a pawn shop for me. And he set to teaching me. I started to imagine what it would be like to be on stage. He was...enthralling. Up there shootin' whiskey between sets with my uncle, all eyes on him when he played. And that man can play. The first time he pulled me on stage, I thought I would piss myself." She laughed at the memory. "I really did. I thought it would be so embarrassing, and I would shame my dad and my uncle. I froze. But my dad didn't let me run off the stage. He just kept playing, and my uncle started singing my part. Eventually, I sang with him, and eventually my uncle let me take over the song. I *loved* music."

"Loved. But not anymore?"

She smiled sadly. "I had this dream that I would find bands like the Beck Brothers and gift the world with real talent. That I would change the industry and give people music that spoke to their souls, not just their pocketbooks."

"And?"

"And I never figured out how to do it. Not in time."

"Juno?" he asked.

"Hmm?"

Rhett's face was so serious and his eyes a dark blue as he asked, "Who's your dad?"

"Brighton Beck."

"Holy fuckin' shit," he said before she'd even finished the last syllable. "I knew it. I knew it had to be him or Dennison Beck when you were talking about how you grew up. Look at this." When he lifted his forearm, it was covered in gooseflesh. "Juno Beck?"

She smiled and sang softly as she strummed the guitar, "That's meeeee."

"Holy fuckin' shit," he repeated, shaking his head in disbelief. "Why didn't you tell me?"

"What does it matter?"

"It matters to me. You said you look up to me, right? You look up to what I was trying to do for the industry and for shifters? Who do you think *I* looked up to? Do my actions remind you of anyone? Your dad and uncle were who I idolized growing up. My Pride was falling apart, my life was falling apart, but I had one thing to focus on." He gestured to her guitar. "Music. And when I was a kid, shifters had just come out and the world hated us, but your dad was making music anyway. Bear shifter, uninterested in fame, recording albums in some hole-in-the-wall studio called..."

He pulled his phone out, punched in some keys, and then laughed and shook his head again. He turned the phone around, and it was a picture of the studio they'd made in the office of Layla and Kong's bar. And there she was in a little blue tutu and ballet shoes, legs crossed on a chair as she frowned down at a coloring book. Her hair was up in curly pigtails and her tongue was sticking out in concentration. She still did that when she was really focused. And there was her dad and Uncle Denny, both playing guitar and singing into a pair of microphones. The picture was an old black and white grainy image, and on the back wall of that makeshift studio was a sign the Ashe Crew had made for them that said *Beck Brothers*.

Rhett pointed to the little girl. "That's you, isn't it?"

She didn't know why she was tearing up. Maybe it was just because she hadn't seen this picture in years, or maybe it was the good memories it brought her, or maybe it was holding a guitar again. "That was in the back of Sammy's Bar. It was the best room for acoustics they could find. My dad and uncle didn't have two pennies to rub together, but they didn't need it. They just did their thing and stayed out of the spotlight and kept the attention on their music. I wanted more of that. And I never saw anything come close…until you."

There was no humor in Rhett's face now. No smile waiting to happen, no wicked glint to his eyes. There was only shock. "You came here. Out of all the mountains, out of all the Crews, you landed on my doorstep."

"Maybe the universe thought we were supposed to meet."

"Your dad… Apex experimented on him, right?"

She nodded. "They took him and my uncle when they were young. They cut out my father's voice box to see if his shifter healing would grow it back." She swallowed down the rage she felt every time she thought about it. "It didn't."

"But he didn't let that stop him from making music."

She smiled and shook her head. "My father is a very strong man. He just didn't know it until my mom came along and pushed him in the right direction."

"Apex made a drug," he said suddenly. "A shifter

can inject themselves, and it'll keep the animal asleep. It has some side effects, though."

She frowned and shook her head. "I...I don't understand."

"I have a sister. She's an addict."

Well, anyone could've knocked her over with a feather right now. "You have a sister?"

Rhett pursed his lips. "A twin sister. Her lioness is white like my animal. Blue eyes and everything. She looks a lot like me. But her animal..." He chewed the side of his lip for a few seconds. "Well, she doesn't have much control. My father is Alpha of the Pride we grew up in, and he wanted us to be perfect. But my sister kept Changing, two, three times a day. And she Turned someone by accident. He had to bring them into the Pride and cover it all up. So he began giving her the drugs Apex made. They call the drug DeClaw. It's not legal or approved by any government sanction. Your animal sleeps, but the side effect is you get high as fuck. And it's addictive. My sister wanted to make my dad proud, and now she's in a rehab center halfway from here to Portland. Guess how many times my dad visited her?"

"Oh my God," Juno whispered.

Rhett looked disgusted. "God didn't have anything to do with what Apex made."

"Is that why you went into hiding?"

Rhett shrugged. "I was out on the road, fighting every agent and label rule, getting the soul sucked out of my music, trying to Change in secret, surrounded by people but completely alone... And while I was out there playing shows, my sister's life was falling apart just so she could keep a place in that damn Pride. She called me one night, and she was crying. You have to understand, Sara never cries. I was sitting on this curb in Tucson, talking on a cell phone with barely any charge left in it, headed to the last show of the tour, and she just...broke down. Told me everything the Pride had been doing, told me all her mistakes with DeClaw. And she said, 'I need help and I don't know who else to ask.' She'd never asked for anything her whole life. All she ever did was give all of herself, try to make everyone happy, and put everyone else first. So...I left the tour, left my manager and team on the tour bus. I took the guitar because Sara had given it to me," Rhett said, pointing to the treasure Juno cradled still. "I hitchhiked all the way to my sister, and I found her a rehab center far away from the Sage

Pride. That's what I'm really doing here."

"That's why you ran." She didn't ask it, just stated it as the realization hit her. He'd left everything on a dime just because his loyalty to his sister was so big. Left. Everything. She couldn't admire a person any more than she did right now.

He nodded once. "That's why I ran. I became Sara's Pride when she couldn't stand on her own. I heard about this last-chance Crew with Grim as the Alpha close to her rehab center, and I thought, why the fuck not? I had no place to stay, no job, no way to access my bank accounts because my fucking team I thought cared about me froze my accounts the second I reneged on my contract. So now I'm a has-been singer turned lumberjack who will do any-fucking-thing for my sister and never have a moment of regret so long as she's all right." He swallowed hard. "And this is the first time I've told anyone that."

And that admission right there—the one that said he'd just opened up to her—demolished any dam that remained.

He didn't realize it, and she would never get the chance to tell him, but he'd just become hers to protect.

"Don't worry," she murmured, strumming a C chord. "You're safe with me. I'll take your secrets to my grave."

TEN

Juno stared at the screen of her phone. It was lined with dozens of text messages from her boss and co-workers at Halfstone Records. She had to find a way to fly out tomorrow or she was fired.

Another text vibrated her phone. *Pick up your fucking phone.*

And then immediately following was an actual phone call from her boss. Which she ignored, because it was midnight and, really, she didn't like being ordered around like this. She'd already told him she would be on a flight tomorrow so *fuck off*.

She'd had the best night she'd had in as long as she could remember. She and Rhett had talked for hours, even sang a couple of Beck Brothers songs together. She'd tried to argue that she wasn't a songbird, but Rhett had disagreed and made it fun and easy to sing with him. Not once had she thought about her phone or the outside world. And when she'd started dozing off on his bed, he patted her leg, moved the flyaway hair from her face, and told her she should get some sleep.

Gentleman.

Did she want him to be a gentleman? He hadn't even tried to kiss her when he'd walked her back to 1010. He'd given her a lopsided sexy smile, tipped his imaginary hat, and sauntered right back to 1009.

Juno glared at the vibrating phone and huffed a frustrated sound, pushed off the bed, and gathered her shower things. As she washed her hair, her head swirled around and around one country crooner niceboy named Rhett Copeland. He was so different than anyone would even guess. He was so, so, sooo much better.

She stepped out of the baby-puke-brown tub onto a soft gray bathmat and then dressed in an oversize sleep shirt and her cutest granny panties because, truth be told, that's all she'd brought or even owned. And then while towel drying her hair, she padded back across the squishy floors to the bed. Out of curiosity, she checked her phone again. Five new texts and another phone call.

Seriously? She'd put her phone down to have a life for a few hours, and this is what happened? A billion missed calls and angry messages?

Death-glaring her phone lying there all smug on her bed, she asked out loud, "What has my life become?"

"I think I feel your pain," Rhett said from the bedroom doorway.

"Aaah!" she yelled, but it wasn't a high-pitched, cute, girly scream. It was deep and growly thanks to her bear.

"Oh my God, you scream like a man."

Juno couldn't even laugh at his tease because she was too busy clutching her hideously oversize Boomer's Beer T-shirt and trying to convince her heart not to catapult from her chest. "You scared me!"

He chuckled and laid his phone next to hers on the bed, and with a knowing look at her, he scrolled through a ton of text messages. "I hate this thing."

Ew, it looked like her phone.

Heart settling a little, she said, "We should burn

them."

"Don't tempt me."

Whoa, he looked good in his sweatpants, no shirt or shoes and wet hair. He smelled like shampoo, and could a person actually get high just looking at another person? His injuries from the fight were nothing but angry red marks and weren't bleeding anymore. Strong man.

"So…I have an admission," he murmured before she could say something stupid and put them on the fast track to awkward-land again.

"Oh, no," she groaned. "Regrets?"

"What?"

"Well, I just had my favorite night in forever, and now you're here to take it back, right?"

"Say that again."

"You're…here…to take it back?"

"Nah." His smile was slow and laced with something. Hope? "Say the first part."

Her cheeks heated as she ducked her gaze, too chicken to look him in the eyes when she murmured, "That was my favorite night."

Rhett hooked a finger under her chin and lifted her gaze to his. "I should've kissed you."

Okay, now she couldn't control the smile if she tried. "Yeah, you should've."

"I was trying not to be a ruiner like my asshole Crew said and be all respectful of you, but then I went back to my place and couldn't sleep and not even a cold shower helped get you off my mind. So...I'm here for this."

Rhett leaned forward and slid his hand to her neck at the same moment his lips pressed against hers. He held her there, mouth moving so gently with hers she got completely lost. It could've lasted hours, or seconds, she didn't know. All she knew was that when they touched like this, the outside world didn't exist and everything simplified.

With a soft smack of his lips, he eased away and rested his forehead on hers, eyes closed. "Just so you know, I don't do this."

"Do what?"

He opened his eyes, and they were as blue as the sky. He shrugged his shoulders. "Care."

Oh, her whole body fluttered with happiness, and now the heat was back in her cheeks again.

This man really liked her.

She leaned into him and kissed him again,

wrapping her arms around his neck. He smiled against her lips, and she giggled and jumped up. The man had good reflexes—he caught her and held her legs around his waist. His stony erection pressed against her just right. Felt so good as she rolled her hips. Rhett let off a soft, sexy growl and eased her onto the bed, ground against her until she was gasping with pleasure. "Rhett," she pleaded as he slid his hand down between them. "More."

His muscles tensed with every rock of his hips, and when he slid his fingertips in through the side of her panties and felt the wetness he'd made there, he let off the sexiest groan she'd ever heard. When he pushed his finger slowly inside her, Juno arched her back against the mattress, dragging her nails up his broad shoulders. His lips went to her neck, and she could feel his teeth there, right at her tripping pulse. So good. More. She wanted more. So she writhed against his touch, soft gasps escaping every time his hand hit her clit. She was so wet, his finger slid into her easily, but still, it wasn't enough.

Nothing mattered when they touched. Nothing outside of them.

She pushed the waistband of his sweats down to

unsheathe his thick erection, which he pressed between her legs. Stupid panties were in the way, but he yanked them farther to the side, pulled his finger out of her, and settled the swollen head of his cock at her entrance. And now she was delirious with need.

He pushed into her by an inch, and then more and more. "Open up for me, Juno."

Arching her spine and throwing her head back, she moaned as he pushed into her all the way. His hand on the back of her neck gripped tight and held her in place as he rammed into her. The other found her breast and massaged it. So sensitive. Her body was so sensitive to him. Close...close... He pummeled into her faster, filling her, his dick so hard and thick.

"Fuck," he gritted out against her neck.

Harder, faster, she was screaming his name now, claws on his back, sinking into his skin, dragging down...

He arched his back and gritted his teeth, growled a monstrous sound as he slammed into her. Then he pulled out slower, slammed in, out slow, his entire body tensing.

She shattered. From the inside out, she shattered. Gripping her tightly, he bucked into her again and held, his dick throbbing deep to match her own release.

They'd lost their minds together tonight. Or found them. He stayed buried in her until she was finished with every pulse of pleasure. Until he'd filled her completely. Until they both lay there in each other's arms, sated and spent.

That was...everything.

When he eased out of her, she thought he would leave. That's what boys did when they got what they wanted, right? And he did leave. To the bathroom where she could hear the water running. As she curled in a happy little ball, she caught a glimpse of herself in the dresser mirror. Hair wild, panties disheveled to the side, goofy smile on her face.

Rhett returned with a washcloth. "What are you doing?" she murmured when he climbed on the bed and pushed her knees apart.

"Cleaning you." He cupped her sex with the warm cloth and looked at her face with an awed look, like she was the most beautiful thing he'd ever seen.

"You're special, Rhett," she said softly.

"To you. I'm something different to you."

And she got it. To the masses, he was a sex

symbol with the voice of an angel and sex appeal for days. He was this unreachable personality they could find on stage or in interviews or award shows on TV. But to her, he was real and flawed and loyal and kind and funny and protective—she smiled as he tossed the cloth into a hamper in the corner—and very thoughtful and sweet.

He turned off the lights, and now was the time, right? Now he would leave? She didn't want him to, so she was happy when he came back to bed and tucked the covers tightly around them, hugged her against his pounding heart.

"Juno?" he asked in a deep, gravelly, sleepy voice in the dark.

"Mmm?" she asked in that in-between spot between awake and asleep.

"I know you think you're going to die, but you won't."

Juno opened her eyes in the dark and inhaled his scent, committing it to memory. "Do you know who Beaston is?"

Rhett swallowed audibly and drew her in closer. It was a full minute before he responded. "Yes, I know who and what he is."

"Good. Then I won't have to explain too much. He was the one who told me I would die in my twenty-seventh year."

"Is he ever wrong?"

She wished with all her heart that her answer could be different, but that wasn't her story. "No. He's never been wrong."

ELEVEN

Rhett scribbled faster in the first rays of dawn. Juno was lying in bed, a soft smile on her lips, her hair wild on the pillow, her leg and arm draped over the other pillow he'd slid there in his place. He hadn't wanted to wake her, but his muse was restless. Whatever magic Juno possessed, she'd woken up the music in him again.

He put the last line down and then stared at it, barely legible on the paper. He'd scratched notes all over it, marked out words and verses to improve them, changed the rhythm of the song twice, but this was it. It felt big. Important.

It was "Juno's Song."

She sighed in her sleep and stretched her long

legs under the covers. It was cold this morning, so he'd gotten up, started a pot of coffee, and put a space heater by the bed, pointing it right at her. He turned and looked at his reflection in the mirror, scrutinizing the long, half-healed claw marks down his back. Did she realize what she'd done?

"You're still here," she murmured in a sleepy voice. God, she was beautiful. Her silver eyes were all crinkled at the corners as she smiled at him. She didn't know it, but a piece of him already lived for that smile. When a man could make a woman smile like that...no power could compare.

He folded the piece of paper and shoved it in his pocket. "I made coffee. And I'm pretty good at scrambled eggs, or we can do a breakfast date in town."

"Gasp," she murmured. "Breakfast, too? Rhett Copeland, are you trying for perma-pussy?"

He blasted a surprised laugh. "Hell, yeah, I am. Get dressed woman. I have something else I want to show you."

"Another big share?"

He nodded as he sat on the bed beside her.

She slid her hand over his knee and squeezed

gently. "What is it?"

"You'll see."

"Ugh, I'm terrible with surprises!"

He snorted when she kicked her legs dramatically under the covers. "Surprises are awesome. You're being ridiculous. Next time remind me to hit it and quit it with you."

Juno smacked his leg, and now he was really laughing.

"I have to go back," she said suddenly.

The laugh died in his throat. "What do you mean?"

"I have to finish what I started. I'm supposed to fly out today to meet a band. I've already committed, and they're all waiting for me to get there. I have the offer and contract for them. It's a big moment for any band and it's something I need to follow through on." She looked like she was going to cry, and he wanted to fix her sadness. "I wish I could just stay here for the rest of my life, but I have loose ends to tie up."

Her words felt like a punch in the gut. Not because they were a betrayal, but because it felt like losing her.

"I'm supposed to be working today, but I can take

you to the airport while we're in town."

She squeezed the fabric of his sweats in her fist. "I'm sorry."

"I have conditions."

"Okay, name them."

"Before we go to the airport, lets treat the day like tomorrow is a million years away."

Her smile appeared, faltered, then appeared bigger as she nodded. "Deal."

Rhett moved to get up and make her coffee because he really did want to do this. He was going to try his damndest to treat today like they had hundreds more ahead of them. She deserved good days, especially if hers were so tightly numbered.

He wanted to be a good memory. The best one, maybe, shoot for the stars and all that shit.

"Hey, Rhett?" she asked before he got to the door.

"You want to give me a blow job? That's what you were about to ask, right?"

Juno giggled. "No, that was definitely not what I was going to ask."

He leaned against the doorframe. "Then what?"

"Someday if I came back here, would this be the same?"

"Are you asking if you mean something to me?"

She nodded.

"You just said no to a blow job, so probably not."

He belted out a laugh as a pillow sailed across the room and hit him square in the chest. He shook his head as he made his way into the kitchen, reveling in her cute giggles.

Crazy girl.

Couldn't she feel it?

Didn't she know what she'd done by marking up his back?

She didn't just mean something.

Now, she meant everything.

TWELVE

"Where do you think you're going?" Remi called from behind them.

Juno winced and gripped the inside of Rhett's bicep harder. She adjusted his guitar case in her hand and turned slowly. "The truth?"

Remi looked like a pissed-off little hellion, her wild black hair waving in the wind and her eyes glowing green, her arms crossed over her chest. "The truth would be nice."

"Honestly, I was hoping to sneak out of here before you saw us and text you to meet us in town for lunch before my flight after I had my suitcase all loaded up and you couldn't trick me into staying."

"Fair enough. Where are we eating lunch?"

Juno narrowed her eyes. That was way too easy.

"Uh, I was thinking the whole Crew could meet at Rusty's Fried Chicken?" Rhett called. "For Crew bonding time that you're always begging us to do."

Remi's dark eyebrow arched up. "Sounds great."

"She looks mad," Rhett said out of the corner of his mouth.

"Yeah, maybe we should go." She lifted her voice to Remi. "Hey, best friend, want to meet us at noon?"

"Sure. How did you book a new flight if your app was down?"

"My boss booked a new one for me. He told me this morning."

"Great. Fuck your boss."

"Remi, you shouldn't have hacked my account in the first place."

"I didn't! Ashlynn and Bash did! I was just the messenger! See you at noon!"

"Good God, woman," Grim barked at Remi from his porch. "Did you get your fuckin' period or something?"

"You shut your murdery mouth, Grim Reaper! Yeah, first and last name!"

"Those aren't my real names."

"You know nothing about friendship so you wouldn't understand!"

"She's going out on a breakfast date with the man she boned!" Grim yelled back, his eyes flashing yellow. "A friend would stop cock-blocking her."

"What is happening?" Rhett whispered, his eyes wide and trained on Grim, whose face was all red and angry. Even his mohawk seemed to be spikier than usual.

"She doesn't have a cock!" Remi shrieked.

"Vagina block then!" Grim yelled back. "Yes or no on your period because you're acting like a psycho."

"Takes one to know one, Count—"

"If you call me Count Psychopotamus one more fuckin' time—"

"Rule number one! I'll state it again because you are a stupid boy but, really, it should be common sense," Remi yelled. "Just because a woman has feelings doesn't mean she's on her period!"

"So, yes?" Grim asked, looking smug. "Because Rhett's been drawing little red raindrops on the Crew calendar every month, and this is day two of girly splish-splash time. I Googled it, and your moodiness should be at maximum—"

"We should leave now," Rhett muttered, backing away from the screaming match.

"You can't put a whole sentence together the entire time I've lived here, and now you're an expert on my menses?" Remi yelled.

"I was trying to be sensitive," Grim said with a shrug.

"Mission not accomplished. Rusty's Fried Chicken at noon. Don't sit by me." Remi leveled Juno and Rhett with a fiery look. "In fact, no one sit by me!" And then she did an about face and slammed the door behind her.

Kamp had come around the corner of the house holding two bottles of beer in his hands. His mouth hung open as he stared at the door Remi had disappeared into.

"That's all yours, man. Congrats," Grim muttered, jogging down the stairs. He yanked an ax out of the wood-splitting log in his front yard and stomped into the woods.

"I'm gonna be late to work today," Rhett called.

The answer "I don't fuckin' care" echoed back to them.

Juno was trying not to laugh, really she was, but

that was awesome. She hadn't seen her best friend that fired up in a long time. There was that passion she knew was in Remi.

Kamp glared at Rhett. "Man, fuck you for putting her in a bad mood. Now I have to sit by myself at the chicken place because I'm sure as hell not sitting by the rest of you."

Juno snickered, imagining them all sitting around the restaurant in separate spots. This was Gray Back behavior. Total C-Team. It was awesome.

Rhett wrapped his hand around hers and tugged her toward the trail that led to the parking field, toting her heavy suitcase with his other hand.

"I thought I was gonna show up here and Remi would be in this delightful, polite Crew, and y'all are so messed up," Juno crowed. She was in full-swing giggles now. "I think Remi will be just fine here."

"She's a pain in everyone's ass," Rhett muttered, but turned a smile on her. "That's why I wanted her to stay."

"Troublemaker."

He wrenched his voice up an octave and repeated Remi's words, "Takes one to know one."

Okay, now she was dying laughing. None of this

should be amusing. Normal Crews and families didn't yell at each other about their periods first thing in the morning. Or drink beer? She hadn't even thought to ask Kamp what he was doing with beer this early. And they didn't all try to kill each other every night, but for some reason these people felt familiar. Not like she'd met them before, but familiar to her heart.

As soon as they were in the truck, Rhett turned on an old country station and started singing along. He kept looking over at her as they drove down the mountain with an encouraging smile until she gave in and was singing along with him. The sunshine had broken through the clouds this morning, and all the new snow was sparkling like God had floofed the world in glitter. The sunrays were filtering through the window, saturating the light on Rhett's profile. Goodness...his smile when he sang. He kept sneaking her glances, too, and his eyes were dancing, sunlight highlighting his white T-shirt so brightly he looked like an angel.

As short as she lived, she was going to remember this. It was bigger than life. It was special.

It was happiness.

Rhett slid his hand over Juno's thigh and drove

with one hand resting on the steering wheel of his old Chevy, never breaking in their car karaoke until he pulled up to a pancake shack. They left her suitcase in the back and got out, chattering all the way inside and to their table. And then they chattered all through breakfast, which was two matching stacks of pancakes big enough to fill their insatiable shifter bellies, complete with slabs of thick-cut bacon, scrambled eggs, and hash browns.

"I'll never be able to eat again," Juno said, leaning back in the chair as Rhett paid the tab. Okay, that was a total lie. She would be hungry again by noon.

Juno frowned when the waitress brought a bag of to-go pancakes to the table. "A snack for later?"

Rhett handed the check to the waitress and told her to, "Keep the change," and then he stood and offered Remi his hand. "Nah. These are for Sara."

Juno slid her hand into his and let him pull her up. He leaned down and kissed her lips. He tasted like syrup, and her bear was purring like an overgrown housecat. After he eased away, he said, "Do you want to meet my sister?"

"I would really love that," she whispered.

Oh, she knew this was a big share for him. He

hadn't exposed Sara to the limelight the entire time he'd been in it. He'd kept her hidden and safe from the chaos of his life. But for Juno…he was letting her in.

The drive to the Safe Oak Rehabilitation Facility was a short one, maybe ten minutes. He held her hand the whole way, and she was glad he'd made the rule that they should act like today wouldn't end. She was reveling in his touch. But as they pulled up to the rehab center, it hit her that her hours here were very numbered. And such an overwhelming sadness washed through her.

She didn't want to leave.

"Come on," he murmured. "I'll have to do a session with her and her doctor first, but she might be ready to meet you right after."

"Okay, don't worry about me. I can just wait in the waiting room and catch up on emails."

"Ha. I bet you have four thousand in there."

"You're probably close," she muttered as she followed him through the front doors.

"I'll be back soon," he said as she took a seat in the waiting area by a rack of magazines.

"Okay," she murmured, watching him disappear

as a nurse buzzed him in through a set of swinging doors.

The second she could no longer see him, the sadness was back, and it was so overwhelming her body physically ached. She wrapped her arms around her stomach and hoped she wouldn't Change. Something was happening to her. Something she didn't understand.

One day with him, and she felt so...different.

THIRTEEN

The second he opened the door, he knew Sara was okay. He could feel it. There wasn't stress coming from her animal, only relief.

Her hair was the same color as his, but down to her shoulders, and her eyes were the same shade of blue. Her smile even looked like his. Dr. Monroe was already seated in his chair and gave Rhett a two-fingered wave.

Rhett made his way to Sara and hugged her up tight, swaying gently. She'd always been a hugger. She was affectionate like their mom.

"You scared the shit out of me yesterday."

Sara shrugged and released him, then yanked the plastic bag of food from his hands and plopped down on the couch. "It was just a little Change. It had been a while, and my animal gets restless all cooped up in this place."

Rhett blinked hard and looked at Dr. Monroe, who wore the same smug look Grim had this morning. "Well, that's a change in attitude. You used to hate Changing."

"Well, it's still not my favorite," she said, pouring a little plastic container of syrup over the pancakes she'd set on the coffee table, but I'm learning to accept that part of myself."

His grin had to be so fucking big right now. He sat next to her and grabbed one of the pieces of bacon out of her Styrofoam container. Munching on it thoughtfully, he relaxed back into the couch. "Has Dad messaged you today?"

"Yes. And Mom."

"Mom did? Wow, I'm surprised she was allowed to use the phone," Rhett said sarcastically. He'd always hated how his mother was treated in the Pride. Like her only value was her albino lion genetics and nothing else.

"A lot has changed in the Pride," Sara said quietly.

"Like what?"

"Like Mom left Dad."

Rhett lurched forward. "What?"

"Yeah. She has her own house on the edge of the territory. She left him when you came and got me, when she found out he'd been giving me DeClaw. When I go back, I'll be living with her until I feel ready enough to have my own place again. She has an extra room all made up for me."

Okay...this was news. Good news, but Rhett still worried. He didn't trust anyone in the Pride except for Mom. "What if you start getting pressure to use DeClaw?" Rhett asked low. Her answer mattered. It had been on his mind since the day he'd taken her from there.

"I like my animal now. I don't want to put her to sleep. I've dealt with my guilt, and I'm still dealing with it. I'm a total work in progress, but I can't stay in here forever. I've been ready to leave for a while."

Rhett held her gaze for a few seconds and then looked to Dr. Monroe.

"I believe she's ready," he said. "She's worked her tail off, she's changed her mindset, and become stronger. I think she can handle it."

"Look, I know what you gave up for me," she

whispered, her eyes brimming with tears. "Music was your escape from the Pride, and you gave that up to take care of me. I don't want to be a burden on your life anymore, Rhett. I want you to move on and grow, too. You can't do that if you're stuck here watching me."

"Well...I don't feel stuck."

Sara frowned. "What do you mean? I thought you said you hated your Crew."

Rhett shrugged up his shoulders. "They're fun to annoy. Tolerable even on some days."

Sara's eyebrows arched up. "Seriously?"

"No, they're terrible. I will leave them any minute now."

Sara snorted and muttered "liar" around a bite of pancakes.

"When are you going back?" he asked suddenly. He was going to miss these visits. It would be different for both of them when she went back to the Saga Pride.

"Dr. Monroe thinks I'll be good to go at the end of the week. He wants me to get one more controlled Change in before Mom picks me up. To build my confidence."

Rhett nodded for a bit and then cleared his throat. "Do you think you're up for meeting someone new?" he asked carefully.

She stopped chewing and gulped a big bite down. "Who?"

"A girl."

"A girl or *the* girl?"

He tried and failed to smile. "I can't keep her."

"Is she here?"

He nodded once.

"Well, bring her on in." She turned to Dr. Monroe. "Can we?"

The thin-haired man shrugged. "I don't see why not."

Rhett stood to get Juno, but Dr. Monroe motioned him down and made a call on the landline phone next to his chair to one of the nurses to bring her back.

Why was his heart pounding so hard right now? Seconds ticked by, and he couldn't keep his eyes from the door. And when it opened, he was struck again with how pretty she was. Her eyes were silver like her animal was riled up, but the smile on her lips was easy. She gave him the cutest fuckin' little wave he'd ever seen. She was so cute when she got shy like that.

"Whoa," Sara uttered beside him. When he looked at Sara, she was smiling, too, right at him.

"What?" he asked.

"The way you look at her..." Sara turned to Juno and made her way around the table to greet her. Rhett thought she would offer her hand for a shake, but his sister pulled Juno into a back-cracking hug and said, "I'm Sara Saga. I've heard so much about you in four sentences."

Juno laughed and hugged her back. "I'm Juno Beck."

"Beck." Sara turned with Juno still locked in her anaconda embrace. "Hey, remember when we were growing up and you were obsessed with the Beck Brothers and had all their posters on your walls? Of course, you would fall for a girl with their last name."

"Brighton Beck is her dad," he deadpanned.

"Holy fuckin' shit!" Sara yelled.

Rhett snorted. She sounded just like him.

Juno was laughing good now. "Your brother had the exact same reaction."

And as he watched his sister and his...Juno...talking and laughing, he thought maybe he'd never had a moment as happy as this one. These two girls were the only ones in the world who had managed to chip away at the cracks in his concrete heart and let themselves in.

No matter what else happened, today was a good day.

FOURTEEN

From experience, Juno knew the only way to make amends with Remi when she was angry like this was a hug. So the second Remi got out of the passenger's side of Kamp's truck, Juno was ready. She pounced. Not gracefully, but she lurched at her friend, wrapped her arms around her, and stood there nuzzling her cheek and trying not to laugh until Remi muttered, "Forgiven," and hugged her back.

Grim mumbled, "Gross," as he stomped out of his navy blue Bronco and right past them.

"He likes me," Remi said in a mushy voice.

"Really?" Juno said, frowning at the behemoth's back. He was wearing a tank top, but it was twenty degrees out. He might be a demon. "How can you tell?"

Was it the growling, the hateful words, the trying to kill them last night, or—?

"Because he showed up."

Huh. Okay then, she supposed that was the benefit of being a monstrous, terrifying asshole. Do one good deed, and ye shall be praised.

Secretly, though, Juno kinda liked that he was grumpy and a little serial-killery. She didn't know what that said about her, but then again, she was dying, so who cared?

She and Rhett followed Kamp and Remi inside. Grim was already sitting at a table, ordering without them. Juno pursed her lips against a smile as Remi griped at him. Rhett's fingertips on the small of her back as she made her way to the table felt so good, and so right. The chairs were wooden bench seats, so she got to sit right in the middle of Rhett and Remi. Grim sat on one side alone, but mostly because when Kamp sat next to him, he snarled. Kamp snarled back and slapped Grim's water glass onto him. They both stood in a rush and nearly faced off right there in Rusty's Fried Chicken. Messes, both of them.

"Ten bucks on Grim," Rhett said without looking

up from his menu.

"Ten on Kamp," Remi said and then slurped her own water.

But before Juno could call out her bet, Kamp rolled his eyes and then sat by Remi. "You're the worst Alpha in the world."

"Agreed," Grim muttered, wiping water off his face with a napkin.

As they all bantered about who could eat the most food and began placing bets on that, Juno got hit in the gut with that awful feeling again. It was the ache of emptiness that came with just a moment of thinking about how it would be when she went back to her old life and left this behind. Her entire body tensed up, and she hunched in on herself.

"Juno, are you okay?" Rhett asked, rubbing her back.

With his touch, the pain disappeared, but something tickled her top lip. Rhett's eyebrows furrowed with a frown, and he pressed a napkin under her nose. When he drew it back, it was dotted with red. "Your nose is bleeding."

It was the sickness. Another sign of Beaston's prediction, and she suddenly wanted to cry because she wasn't ready. Before, she'd accepted it. She'd gone balls to the wall with work to get as much done in the time she knew she had. But now, everything had changed.

She wasn't ready to die.

"It's okay," Rhett murmured, hugging her close to his side. He smelled like fur, and when she looked up, his eyes were icy blue.

"What's wrong?" Remi asked.

"I have a confession," Rhett said without missing a beat. "I have a sister a couple towns over who is finishing up rehab. She's been wanting to meet all of you, and she's leaving at the end of the week so you should probably meet her now. While you can. Because she's going back to the Saga Pride and they're all recluses and she'll probably never get out of that cult again."

Remi and Kamp both sat there staring at him like he'd lost his damn mind, but Grim was chuckling as he looked from face to face and chewed on a cornbread muffin. "Y'all are so fucked up."

"Why didn't you tell us you had a sister?" Remi asked. "I've asked you like six times about your family, and you've only answered, 'Does not compute.' And you've been talking to her about us?"

"Oh, yeah," Rhett said, smearing butter on a cornbread muffin. "All bad stuff."

"What the hell, man?" Kamp asked. "Do we seriously not know each other at all?"

And then another argument was off to the races.

Under the table, Rhett squeezed her leg comfortingly. Clever man.

Just like that, Rhett had distracted everyone away from asking any more in-depth questions about what was wrong with her.

FIFTEEN

Goodbyes had never bothered Juno before. They just hadn't. She'd never drawn them out or overthought them. She was just tough about see-ya-laters.

Today was different.

Everything was different.

She hadn't checked her phone while she'd waited to meet Sara. Hadn't checked it in the truck on the way to Rusty's. Hadn't checked it while the Crew ate lunch together. Perhaps that was because the conversations were so funny and interesting, but she knew it was more than that. Her life used to be staring at the glowing screen of her phone, building her career. But one day of an actual break from it, and she felt happier, steadier. And for that single day, she'd actually lived.

Kamp and Grim and Remi had said their goodbyes in the parking lot of Rusty's Fried Chicken. She'd teared up. For the first time ever, she'd teared up on a goodbye, and it wasn't just for Remi either. It was for the wild boys who would go on arguing and bleeding each other in those mountains long after she was gone. Life would go on here, and she would not. And missing a single moment of "living" made that ache come back again in waves.

"I understand you have to finish what you started," Rhett said from the driver's seat. His hands gripped the wheel so hard his knuckles had turned white. "You're a special kind of woman. You see things through." He sighed and arched his bright blue gaze to her. "But this morning I wished on that dumb house number that you would stay."

"You wished on 1010?"

"Remi said it works sometimes. I poked my finger right in the middle of one of the zeros and pretended it was your boob. Then I made the wish."

"You're not supposed to say the wish out loud or it won't come true."

Rhett frowned at the car parked in front of them in the airport passenger unloading zone. "Won't come true anyway. I don't believe in that stuff, and look at you."

Indeed, she was cradling her suitcase in her lap. Her lip was trembling, and she was going to lose it again. Rhett shoved open his door and got out, walked around the front of the truck, and opened her door for her. He helped her settle the suitcase on the sidewalk and pulled his guitar case out of the bed of the pickup.

"I want you to have something from me."

Juno nearly choked on nothing. "W-what? No, Rhett, I can't take your guitar."

"A gift for a gift, and it's the only material thing in the world that means anything to me."

"A gift for a gift? What did I give you?"

Rhett gave her a sad smile and turned around. Slowly, he lifted his shirt up to expose deep healing slashes down his back. "Claiming marks."

And Juno...the girl who prided herself on being tough, the girl who prided herself on being strong, lost it right there in front of that airport. Twin tears raced down her cheeks, and her shoulders shook as she clasped her hand over her mouth to keep her sobs all caged up.

She had done that, hadn't she? How had she not realized? How had she not thought of what she was doing when they were together? Her bear had taken over that part of her story and tried to tell her, "This man is mine." But she'd been so consumed by the chaos of the day and the implications of her sickness that she hadn't realized just what she'd done.

Claiming marks looked different for everyone, but they could never be shoved under the rug and excused away. Thinking back, her bear had known just what she was doing.

She'd claimed Rhett.

"I can't..." He swallowed over and over, rubbing his hand down the scruff on his jaw. There was heartbreak in his eyes. "I can't watch you cry, or I'm gonna lose my pride and beg you to stay. You make me happy, and it's been a long damn time. I thank you for that. Come back if you get bored with that old life. Okay, Juno?"

She couldn't answer. All she could do was nod her head once before he bolted for his truck. He didn't look back at her until he was pulling away, and the hurt in his eyes made her squat down next to his guitar and hate herself for doing this to them.

And as she rested her hand on that old guitar, the instrument that had known real love and real music, the dam that had broken and freed the water also freed her. A small splat sounded against the ground, and then another and another.

It wasn't only her tears that painted the concrete as she watched Rhett's taillights disappear.

Her nose was bleeding again.

Her time was running out, and the reasons for her to leave for even a night were evaporating one by one. Everything that had once been important didn't seem to matter, and everything that hadn't mattered before meant everything to her now.

Somehow, that man had broken her together again.

She'd been searching for him her whole life and hadn't even known it, and the second she'd seen him, her soul had recognized his.

And right then and there, she swore to herself she would finish what she had to and come back home before the end of her days.

Because that's what Rhett was.

Home.

SIXTEEN

This was pop music, not country like the Beateaters had labeled themselves. It was catchy, the lyrics were easy, and every song sounded exactly the same. With the right marketing team, their debut album would probably sell a ton.

Juno sat in the back of the smoky bar, wincing against the pyrotechnics and flashing lights, surrounded by people who couldn't take their eyes off the Beateaters. She'd sat through their entire set, but her head hurt and her heart wasn't in it. It was back in a little trailer park in Rogue Pride territory that she'd left yesterday.

She couldn't wait for tonight to be over.

"Look at this!" a girl beside her exclaimed. She

was staring at the glowing screen of her phone and leaned over to her friend to show her. Probably a picture of a cat playing piano or something.

Oh, good grief, the Beateaters were getting a standing ovation. They weren't done. Juno gritted her teeth and clutched her satchel with the contract, counted to five for patience.

There was murmuring around her, though, and people weren't as enthralled with the band as they had been. Couples and trios were staring at their phones and whispering to each other.

Annoyed, she finally asked the girl next to her, "What's going on?"

"Rhett Copeland. He's playing at some bar!"

"What?" she said, her voice wrenching up an octave. "Can I see?" She pulled the girl's phone to her. "Is this live?"

"Yeah! It's streaming live. He's at some bar called Sammy's."

What the fucking fucking fucking fuck? The video was shaky, and the bar was crowded and dark. Looked just the same as she remembered it. Dark wood floors and old street signs on the walls. On the stage where her father had played a hundred concerts sat Rhett. Just him on a single stool, with another stool beside him serving as a tabletop a bottle of whiskey and a shot glass. He wasn't playing his guitar because she had it. Instead, he was playing the old guitar her father had bought her from the pawn shop all those years ago.

She teared up the second he leaned toward the microphone. He didn't look nervous at all. His smile was easy and relaxed, and the gray T-shirt he wore clung to him just right. It was V-neck, and he wore a couple of thin leather necklaces. His belt was made of worn leather, his jeans had holes in the knees, and his hair was messed up just right.

"This is a song I wrote a couple days ago," he said into the mic, his voice deep and sexy. "I met this girl, and she loosened up my muse. And I'm gonna ramble here for a moment, but y'all…my muse was a mess for a while. So me being able to hear a song in my head again…well, that's a big deal to a dried-up songwriter. And I owe it to her." He looked right into the camera and said, "Juno Beck, I'm in your hometown. I talked your dad into letting me use your guitar tonight since you have mine. It's waiting here for you. Come on, get it, girl."

Someone in the audience yelled, "Or come get *him!*"

He chuckled and lifted a shot of whisky with a wink. "Yeah, what that guy said. Or come get me, Juno. I'm gonna play here every night until you walk through that door." He grinned at the audience. "Are y'all ready to hear some music?"

The crowd was so loud it made the sound go staticky. The girl next to her was leaning over her shoulder, watching it with Juno. "God, whoever he is talking to is so lucky."

Oh, that girl had no idea just how lucky.

Rhett took the shot of whiskey during the cheering, set it down neatly on the stool next to him, and gripped the neck of the guitar. He closed his eyes, and then he sang the first line of a song, his deep baritone voice with that southern accent ringing out clear as a bell. The crowd went still.

The first time I saw her standin' there, I knew I was done
She was the one
Gonna wreck the wild right outta me.

He strummed the guitar on the last word and the crowd turned into a chorus of girl-screams.

Juno sat there watching the video of him playing, from the first word to the last of the song. He was mesmerizing. Around her, the world didn't exist. It was just her and Rhett, and he was singing right to her. When he finished the song, he told the audience, "That one's called 'Juno's Song.'"

The cheering was deafening. God, what she would give to feel the energy of that place right now. Because that's what music did. It healed the heart and spoke to something deeper than the mind. She knew Rhett was filling that room with joy tonight and giving people a concert they would never forget.

The next song was his biggest hit, the one everyone in Sammy's would know. And they did. They sang every word, the lights on their cell phones held up high and swaying as Juno sat there watching in a bar hundreds of miles away, tears streaming down her face, so damn proud of him.

This...this was what she'd gotten into the industry for. This is what she remembered from her childhood.

This was the important grit.

Chills rippled up her arms on the first line of the next song. It was a tribute to the great old singers of country. He stopped mid-song to lift a shot to the crowd, and they kept singing for him while he took the shot. He closed his eyes, bobbed his head, and played guitar for his audience, leaned into the mic a few lines later and picked it back up for them at the chorus.

He was doing it acoustic—his whole set.

No drums, no lights show, no tambourine, no extras. Just him and an acoustic guitar making magic happen in an old bar that had built her. Stripping it back down to the basics—an instrument and a voice.

She'd been doing this wrong, hadn't she?

She'd been trying to change the industry, searching for someone with that it-factor to feed to a big label so they could get their songs to the masses.

But look what he was doing.

"Hey, Juno!" Timothy, the lead singer for the Beateaters, greeted her.

"Juno?" the girl whose phone she was using asked. "*The* Juno? Juno Beck? The Juno that Rhett Copeland is singing to?" Her voice was super high-pitched right now.

Juno handed back her phone. To Timothy, she said, "That was a great show. You've been working really hard as a band and Halfstone Records would like to offer you a contract." She pulled the thick stack of papers from her satchel along with a pen and handed them to Timothy. Behind him, his bandmates were freaking out. As they should be. This was a big deal. They really had worked hard to get where they had. This just wasn't her place and didn't speak to her heart. "Let your lawyers look over it. Negotiate if it's something that means a lot to you, and when it's signed, send it back to Manny Drummund at Halfstone Records. The address is on this envelope along with the postage." She shook Timothy's hand, and then his bandmate's one by one.

"Wait, where are you going?" Timothy asked. "Party with us tonight! We're celebrating! You made this happen!"

"Oh, you don't need me to celebrate. You did this for yourselves. Congratulations. I have a flight to catch."

The girl near her squealed. "To go see *him*, right? To go get your guitar back from Rhett Copeland?"

Juno winked at her and picked up the handle of

Rhett's guitar case. She hadn't let it out of her sight since he'd given it to her. Her nose didn't bleed if she had it with her. It had become her friend. Juno made her way out of the bar, smiling as the murmurings behind her got louder. Rhett's reappearance was spreading like wildfire, and apparently so was the mention of her, because a few people followed her out of the bar, taking pictures. Of her? Why? She hadn't done anything. Rhett was the magic one.

And as she made her way to her rental car, the emptiness that had sat like a bowl of cement in her center filled up. She was making her move. She was doing what she'd been meant to do all along. She just hadn't been able to see it.

Guitar tucked in the passenger's seat, Juno answered her vibrating phone. It was Manny.

"You knew where Rhett Copeland was?" he yelled. "And you didn't tell us? You didn't sign him? You didn't do anything about it?"

"I gave the Beateaters their contract. I think they'll sign."

"Rhett! Copeland!"

"Hey, Manny? I quit."

"What?"

"I *really* fuckin' quit." God, it felt good to say that. The emptiness was completely demolished now. She'd gone out on her own terms, followed through with her commitments, finished her job. It was a loose end that she'd needed to tie up before the end, and she'd tied the hell out of it.

"What are you gonna do?" Manny demanded.

Juno grinned and started the car. "I'm gonna go live while I can."

SEVENTEEN

Sammy's Bar hadn't changed a bit. Still had the same gravel parking lot, same old street lights. Same door she'd walked through a hundred times before. The parking lot was full, and not just the lot, but all along the main drag as far as she could see. Cars were shoved in any open space. Outside, there were crowds gathered, probably because Sammy's had reached capacity inside. But the crowd didn't seem to mind. They were bundled up, standing around outdoor heaters, watching a big canvas screen on the side of the building. Music hummed from inside and outside, the video feed matching the lyrics. They were streaming a live feed out here to the people who couldn't fit inside.

Kong and Layla had upped the technology of this place. Nice.

She recognized a few old friends from Damon's Mountains and waved to them as she made her way to the door. She expected Kong, the old silverback gorilla shifter whose mate owned the bar, to be running security, but another familiar face was there instead.

Don't lose it, don't lose it.

Brighton Beck was standing there, tall as an oak and wide as a barn, dark eyes dancing as he watched her approach.

"Hi Dad," she murmured.

As he hugged her, he said in a forced whisper, "Hi, Juno-Bug."

"Were you in on this?"

Dad smiled wickedly and shrugged. "I like him."

She giggled. "Me too."

"His Crew is crazy."

Now she was really laughing. "Agreed. Are they here?"

Dad nodded, kissed the top of her head, and then let her in the door.

The place was packed, but everything melted

away the second she locked eyes on Rhett. And, oh, his smile. He stopped mid-song. "Holy shit, y'all, there she is."

The crowd turned to her and erupted in cheering. She knew some of them. Vyr was here, and Damon, Uncle Denny, Kellen, Tagan, Clinton, Kirk, Bash, Mason, Haydan. All their mates, too. It seemed like everyone had come down from Damon's Mountains for this.

Home. Home. Home was here in Rhett's smile.

"Damn, you're a sight for sore eyes, woman," Rhett said into the microphone. "I fuckin' missed you."

"Awwwwwwwww!" came a few dozen girl voices at once.

"Booooo," Grim called from the bar.

"Yeah, boooo and barf," Kamp called, cupping his hands around his mouth.

Remi was beside him cracking up.

"I have the worst friends in the world," Rhett said with a chuckle. "Juno!" He squinted under the stage lights at her. "Whatcha got there?"

She lifted his guitar case. "A trade," she called.

"Atta girl. I have a surprise for you, and for all of

y'all tonight. A couple of special guests who wanted to come show this good ol boy how it's done."

Juno frowned as the crowd cheered. And then she saw them. Dad and Uncle Denny were making their way to the stage.

"Oh my gosh," she whispered under her breath as they pulled their old guitars off the stands against the wall and climbed up onto the stage with stools in hand. Rhett was pouring them three shots of whiskey. Dad and Uncle Denny gave him bro hugs, and as they settled onto their own stools, Rhett leaned into the mic again. "I grew up with my eyes on one inspiration, and this is a dream come true for me tonight, playing with the Beck Brothers. Now, Juno's dad told me her favorite song, one he wrote for her mother, Everly. This one's called 'Goodish Intentions.'"

The crowd went nuts, and suddenly Mom appeared right beside her. She already had tears in her eyes. Juno leaned into her side hug and rested her head on Mom's shoulder as the boys began to play the song that had most touched her heart as she'd grown up. This song is what had made her believe in love.

She swayed with Mom the whole song, laughing as the occasional tear fell, and reveling in the sound of a hundred voices lifting to sing along.

This was everything.

She could die happy now because this moment had existed for her. Watching her mate, her Rhett, play a song with her dad and Uncle Denny, his eyes drinking her in as he sang right to her soul, like nobody else in this bar existed.

"He's a good one, isn't he?" Mom asked.

"Well, instead of calling me and asking me to come back, he came all the way to the place that means the most to me and made it special again. Plus, he dragged their wild asses here," she said, gesturing to the Rogue Pride Crew. God, she couldn't even imagine them on a plane together. Grim was definitely about to get into a bar fight with everyone. "That alone is a giant effort. I think that's what it's about—the effort." Saying I love you was one thing, but showing love? Now that was entirely different. Maybe it was even bigger than the words.

"I think you're gonna be just fine, Juno-Bug."

Juno smiled sadly. "I wish I had more time with him."

"Now you do," Beaston rumbled from behind her. Remi was standing with him, two shots of something strong-lookin' in her hands.

Green eyes blazing, Beaston held two pictures in his hands. When she hesitated to take them in her confusion, he shoved them forward at her.

"You were always gonna die in your twenty-seventh year. I told you this."

"Yeah," she said, frowning at the picture on top. It was of a magazine clipping. She remembered this. A music mag had interviewed her to get insight on up-and-coming bands and what they needed to do to get signed. The picture was of her, sitting at a two-person table in a pantsuit, watching a band. Her eyes were totally dead. She'd hated that band and signed them anyway.

Beaston pointed to that picture. "She died."

Juno frowned and looked up at him. "I...I guess I don't understand."

He pulled that top picture away and exposed the one underneath. It was her yesterday, outside the bar where the Beateaters had played, mid-stride, holding Rhett's guitar case. She had worn a black ripped-up tank top, shredded black jeans, and heeled booties because she'd felt good about herself and wanted to be comfortable last night. Her leather necklaces were swinging in the breeze, and her hair was lifted on one side...but that smile on her face was what took up the whole, grainy, black and white picture.

"This girl was born," he growled, pointing to that picture. Beaston studied her face with those unsettling green eyes that saw so much more than anyone could fathom. "Happy birthday, Juno."

"What?" she whispered, tears burning her eyes. "I'm not..." She swallowed hard and looked at Remi, then back to Beaston. "I'm okay?"

"You were dead inside, and now you're alive," he said and then melted into the crowd, leaving Juno with a hundred emotions rushing her at once.

"But...my nose was bleeding," Juno whispered to Remi, not ready to believe all her worries were through. She had questions! "And I had an accidental Change and got disoriented."

"Well, yeah, the altitude is way different in Rogue Pride Territory," Remi said. "I got nose bleeds, too, when I first got out there. And your bear was probably wanting to stay, am I right?"

Her mind racing, Juno nodded.

"Yeah, your animal is going to act up if you try to leave her new territory. She picked a place and a mate, and you made her leave." Remi shrugged. "If I was her I would do way worse than bloody noses and accidental Changes."

All Juno could do was stare. She wasn't capable of handling such an overwhelming feeling of reprieve. She parted her lips to try to say something smart, but once again, she Juno-ed it. "Living is awesome."

Remi snorted. "You're dang right it is. Here, shoot this." She handed her a shot.

Feeling like her heart was going to eject itself out of her chest, she could only nod and toss it back with Remi.

Rhett's charming voice rang out clear over the speakers. "I'm gonna take a quick break and go kiss my girl. Is that all right with y'all?"

The crowd cheered, and a few brave or drunk ones, whichever, started chanting, "Kiss her! Kiss her!"

Completely overwhelmed in the best way, Juno made her way toward him, weaving through the crowd as he hopped off the stage. The audience cleared the last few yards that separated them and she ran for him, her Rhett.

He caught her, of course. He was good at that—catching her. And as he brushed her hair from her face, he looked at her like she was the air, and not the other way around.

And when his lips pressed to hers, the crowd went nuts. She smiled the whole way through that kiss, and so did he. Hugging her so tight, letting her feet dangle, he nipped her lip and eased back, looked her right in the eyes and said, "I quit this industry unless you produce my records."

"What?"

The label will take all my money for breach of contract, but I don't give a single fuck. You're the reason I love this again. You're the reason…I…love. Start a label, produce me, let's live like we have ten thousand days left."

She cupped his cheeks and tried her best not to bust out crying, but the dam was nothing but rubble now. All she could do was nod because her voice would break on her answer.

"Yeah? Is that a yes?"

She nodded again as the tears started falling. "You gave music back to me, too."

The smile on his lips fell, but then came back softer. "I know what that really means."

"Tell me."

"You love me."

Oh, she did. She *really* did. "How did you know?"

He kissed her once more. "Because I feel the same."

EPILOGUE

"From the top," she said from behind the glass. "It's close but not quite there. Maybe hold that last note a second longer."

"Yep," Rhett drawled, adjusting his guitar.

"One, two…one, two, three, four," Uncle Denny murmured, and he and Dad began strumming together in the background.

Rogue Rebel Records was now a thing, and they had three days to record an album before Vyr was demanding them back home.

This was her life, and it was a beautiful one. The last couple of days had been chaos, but so fulfilling she didn't miss her old life at all.

Everything made sense now. They were going to

release these songs for cheap, just to get them into listeners' headphones. No gimmicks or high-tech equipment. Guitars, mics, and a whole lot of heart, back here in the office of Sammy's where the Beck Brothers had produced all their albums. It suited Rhett. He was happy, and the new songs were flowing out of him. He was hitting his stride with these songs since no one was telling him what to do or how to write them anymore.

He was in control, and he was flourishing right in front of her. A total pro.

She was so damn proud of him.

Maybe they would sell one record or thousands. They didn't know and they didn't care. They were in this for the music, for the audience, for that feeling in their souls that they were making something special.

"That's it," she said into the mic with the biggest grin. "Nailed it. That's exactly what it needed."

"Okay," Remi said from where she'd been going over numbers with Kong on how much Pen15 Juice beer she and Kamp could get him in two weeks. "Now go in there with him. I want to take a picture."

"What? No, I don't need a picture of me."

Remi held up her phone, and on the screen was

the pic of her as a little kid in this very room, coloring while Dad and Uncle Denny recorded. They'd kept the sound of the scratch of her crayons in that song.

Juno smiled at the memory. "You want to recreate it?"

"Nah," Remi said. "I want to improve it."

And so Juno made her way into the recording studio. She tried to sit next to Rhett, but he wouldn't have it. He pulled her onto his lap, and before she even settled from her laughing, Remi snapped a picture on her phone. And when she showed her, Juno's heart swelled.

She was mid-laugh, and so was Rhett as he looked at her. Dad and Uncle Denny were grinning in the background, holding their guitars under the Beck Brothers, Rhett Copeland, and Rogue Rebel Records signs the Ashe Crew had made and added to the room.

Whatever filter Remi had used made the picture look grainy and old, as if it had been taken all those years ago.

And as Juno and Rhett stared at the picture, she knew pieces of her really had died in her twenty-seventh year. But her favorite parts lived on and were growing. Perhaps love did that, or perhaps it was finding something she was truly passionate about, she didn't know. All she knew was the day she'd found Rhett, he'd changed the course of her entire life for the better.

A home. A place. A niche. A great love. A story. A life worth living.

He'd given them all to her.

A gift for a gift, he'd once said. He'd thought it was the guitar, but she saw it differently.

He'd gotten her living again.

And that was the greatest gift of all.

Want more of these characters?

The Daughters of Beasts series is a standalone series set in the Damon's Mountains Universe.
More of these characters can be found in the following series:

Saw Bears

Gray Back Bears

Fire Bears

Boarlander Bears

Harper's Mountains

Kane's Mountains

Red Havoc Panthers

Sons of Beasts

About the Author

T.S. Joyce is devoted to bringing hot shifter romances to readers. Hungry alpha males are her calling card, and the wilder the men, the more she'll make them pour their hearts out. She werebear swears there'll be no swooning heroines in her books. It takes tough-as-nails women to handle her shifters.

She lives in a tiny town, outside of a tiny city, and devotes her life to writing big stories. Foodie, wolf whisperer, ninja, thief of tiny bottles of awesome smelling hotel shampoo, nap connoisseur, movie fanatic, and zombie slayer, and most of this bio is true.

Bear Shifters? Check

Smoldering Alpha Hotness? Double Check

Sexy Scenes? Fasten up your girdles, ladies and gents, it's gonna to be a wild ride.

For more information on T. S. Joyce's work,
visit her website at
www.tsjoyce.com

Made in the USA
Coppell, TX
26 August 2023